Nuri Does Not Exist

 SADRU JETHA

Talonbooks

Talonbooks
Box 2076, Vancouver, British Columbia, Canada V6B 3S3
www.talonbooks.com

Typeset in Adobe Caslon and printed and bound in Canada.
Printed on 30% post-consumer recycled acid-free paper.

First printing: 2011

The publisher gratefully acknowledges the financial support of the Canada
Council for the Arts; the Government of Canada through the Book Publishing
Industry Development Program; and the Province of British Columbia through
the British Columbia Arts Council and the Book Publishing Tax Credit for our
publishing activities.

Library and Archives Canada Cataloguing in Publication

Jetha, Sadru
 Nuri does not exist / Sadru Jetha.

ISBN 978-0-88922-655-5

 I. Title.

PS8619.E85N87 2011   C813'.6   C2010-907143-3

In Memory
of
Gulshan

아이들

Contents

Nuri Does Not Exist

Father answers to the call of Gulu but his real name starts with the letter *K*. Uncle answers to the call of Hassan but his real name starts with the letter *F*. And Leli Aunty's real name starts with the letter *Z*.

"Why, Grandma?" I ask as we sit cross-legged facing each other on my hard bed.

"Evil spirits, *beta*," she says, hands up undoing her horse-tail bun.

I get up and go behind her.

"It is to confound evil spirits who might wish to harm my children."

My hands close on hers. She slides them out from under mine. I press one hand on the bun and with the other pull out her hairpins, first one, then another, then two more.

"But how, Grandma?"

She shakes her head, runs her fingers through hennaed hair.

"Shush, *beta*, we don't talk about evil spirits at night."

I give her the puff bun and four pins. She tucks them under her pillow.

"Tomorrow then," I say as I move to stand by her side. She presses me close, sandalwood scent.

"You will wake me, Grandma?"

A last squeeze. "To sleep, *beta*."

I sit down on the bed again, facing her. She closes her eyes. "*Bismillah* ... In the name of Allah," she begins her whisper. Then silence, only lips moving, hands folded in her lap.

I look out the window. Moonless stars, thousands. *Nkhuuu*, someone clearing their throat in the distance. Kakoo the grocer's night watchman. Does he really stay awake all night?

"Ali, Ali, Ali," she breathes out, opening her eyes. Her prayer is over. She blows gently, first across my right shoulder and then my left.

"There, *beta*, both the angels on your shoulders protect you now."

I lie down, face turned toward her.

"Sleep in peace, *beta*."

She continues sitting on the bed cross-legged, closing her eyes again, right cheek bulging with the last paan of the day, murmuring, then silent, then blowing to the right and to the left of her shoulders. "Ya Allah," she sighs and lies down next to me. I get closer to her, curl my leg against her bony thighs, arm resting against her spongy belly, smell her sandalwood smell.

When I stretch my arm across the mattress, she is not there. She did not wake me. I jump out of bed, look around. Everyone else in the room except Grandma is fast asleep in their beds, Grandfather with his mouth open, brother Sham babbling in his sleep, sister Faiza curled up round her long pillow. Down one flight of wooden stairs. Gentle snore from Father and Mother's room. Down another flight of stairs to the shop, three steps at a time. She is on her low stool.

"Why did you not wake me?"

She does not look up but reaches for her brass plate, with betel leaves wrapped in wet cloth and three little tin boxes, one for chopped betel nuts, one for bitter white lime paste and one for tasteless brown paste. Chewing tobacco in the little handkerchief, knotted, is in the middle of the plate. I sit on the floor, arms round my drawn-up knees, watching, while she prepares her early-morning paan.

"Could not sleep, *beta*. Got up early. Very early," she says, straightening a leaf on the shiny plate. Rubs on it, with her right forefinger, first the white paste, then the brown, then licks her finger.

"But how, Grandma?"

She adds betel nuts. Folds the leaf three times. Thumb and forefinger lift the tiny bundle. It disappears into her red mouth. I wait for her eyes to close as she takes her first slow bite into the paan, pressing out its sharp juices. She sucks in a deep breath, opens her eyes on me.

"How what, *beta*?" she asks, mouth full.

"How are the evil spirits confounded?" passing her the spittoon under the stool. Cleaned to a shine every night by old Mama Ayah.

She holds it some distance from her, squeezes her lips into *O*. *Puuutsch*, twang. Her first thwack into the spittoon. Places it a few feet away to catch her squirts, short and sharp, for the rest of the day. A straight shooter. Comes with long years of experience, Mama Ayah says.

Though I am five, almost, and in standard one, she lifts me into her lap. I lie facing up. My right hand on her jaw, feeling the quick movement of toothless gums mashing into the paan. She shifts the bulge to the right of her mouth. It will rest there until lunchtime, getting smaller, finally invisible. Her mouth no longer moves, so I drop my hand.

⌘   ⌘   ⌘

Mama Ayah sits on the soft grass under the cool dark of the mango tree. A black silken *bui bui* hides all but her bare feet, hands and face. She is still as air, eyes distant, blade of grass between teeth. I follow the long line of ants starting from the small hole under the flame tree. They are black. Not *majimoto*, the fat red ones which draw blood. Each carries a tiny load. Going … where?

I look up. The sun is not too hot, not so high as at noon. Her eyes are fixed on me, unseeing. I crawl into the salt breeze, over to her, stand across her legs stretched out on the ground. My hands on her cheeks, face nearing hers. Our noses meet.

"Maamaa," I breathe into her mouth.

"*Mwanangu*, my child," she stirs. Presses me hard into her breast. Heavy musk heartbeats. I remove part of the *bui bui* covering her head. It falls on her shoulders. My fingers move along the parting of her plaited woolly hair, fuzzy.

"What does *labek* mean, Mama?"

She turns me round. Lifts me the way Grandma does and lowers me into her lap. Over by the coconut palms is a man, tall and thin, not as black as Mama Ayah. He is binding his ankles with a cord. His hair curls, not as woolly as hers, not straight as mine.

"Mamaaa. *Labek.* Tell me what *labek* means?"

The man leaps onto the grey trunk of the coconut palm. Feet together. Arms gripping the slender trunk. A looping caterpillar.

"It is like this, *mwanangu*," her dry hand stroking my forehead. I place my hand on hers. She stops.

Now at the top of the tree, removing the heavy knife from his loin cloth. *Oonh. Whack.* Thud of a coconut. *Oonh, whack. Oonh, whack. Thud, thud.*

"Yes, *mwanangu*," she starts, removing her hand from my head.

He replaces the heavy knife. Slides down the swaying trunk. Collects the coconuts into a woven basket. Swings it onto his head.

"It is when the master calls his slave."

"By his real name?"

"And the slave replies, *labek*, I come, I obey."

"Did Grandma ...?"

He looks at us, smiles and waves his hand. Mama Ayah waves back. "*Heri*, good fortune, Bilajina."

I say, "*Kwa heri*, goodbye, Bilajina."

Bilajina. Without Name. They found him under the upside down *mbuyu* tree, where the spirits meet at midnight, at noon as well. Not far from where Mama Ayah lives. They waited for his mother to come and claim him. She never came. Some say nobody in the whole of Zanzibar knows his real name. Mama Ayah does not agree. "Allah knows," she says.

"Did Grandma," I begin to ask once again but her arms close in, hard, hurting.

⌘ ⌘ ⌘

"So how are evil spirits confounded, Grandma?"

"It is like this, *beta*," she begins, stroking my hair with her right hand. Her left hand fits into mine. "If an evil spirit wishes to harm you, he has to know your real name. If he doesn't know it, he can't find you."

Her mouth moves again, once. She looks down at me, eyes deep bright. She does not smile.

"And so we call you Nuri. If the evil spirit harms Nuri, well, Nuri is not your real name. The one called Nuri does not exist. And so the real you is unharmed."

"But Nuri is also a girl's name, is it not?"

"So much the better to confuse the spirits."

She looks at me again. She is clever. Didn't Grandfather say that he would be lost without her? When I grow up, I will give not one but several names to my children, none of them real. That should take care of even the cleverest of spirits. I could call one of them Bilajina. Or give them no names at all.

"What does my real name mean?"

Her hand is brown, chickpea, like mine.

"Servant of Allah. But you mustn't tell it to anyone. An evil spirit passing by may hear it."

"Not even during daytime?"

"No, not even then."

I turn her hand. Blue veins soft twisting snakes.

"Why did you name me Nuri?"

She closes her eyes. When she opens them on me, they are shiny sharp. She lifts me roughly, presses me hard against her. Her heartbeats strong as Mama Ayah's. She pulls me back. And then … too late. Her mouth crushes against my ear, muffling her reply, "Because you are the light of my eyes. Hee, hee, hee, hee."

I wipe the wet from my ear. Frowning, I settle back into her lap, curled up hard against her stomach, feeling the laughter inside. She begins stroking my hair again.

⌘   ⌘   ⌘

I am in standard eleven now. An urgent message for me, the headmaster says. I am wanted at home. I run all the way, dodge *homali* carts, cyclists, push through crowds, rush up the wooden stairs and enter Grandma's room. She is propped against two pillows in her hard bed, tired, except for two glints that are her eyes. Father and Mother are kneeling by her bedside. They get up, make way for me.

"I have been waiting for you, *beta*," she complains weakly, paan in mouth.

I enter her raised embrace. Sandalwood scent. Her lips, limp, press against mine. I do not wipe the wet from my mouth. Right hand strokes my hair. Her lips move, then narrow, then blow towards me.

"She's getting weaker," Mama Ayah whispers. She is standing by the wall. Brother Sham and sister Faiza are by her side, lips moving in silent prayers.

"Help me in, *beta*."

I do.

"Cover me, *beta*."

I do.

"Remember the things I told you, *beta*."

She reaches out. I take her hand in mine. Her eyes, still on me, begin to close. She smiles, then heaves up, eyes rolling upwards.

"*Labek*," she cries. Her hand is limp.

"From Him we come, to Him we return," Mama Ayah murmurs from behind me.

⌘ ⌘ ⌘

IMPORTANT.
All persons entering the Colony and Protectorate of Kenya.
Disembarking passengers are required to report to the
Immigration Officer under Immigration Regulations,
section x, subsection y, subsubsection z.
They are required to complete the form prescribed by the
Minister under the aforementioned regulations and present
it to the Immigration Officer.

PENALTY.
False statements will result in prosecution leading
to a fine or imprisonment or both.

The same slip of a form, Grandma.

NAME.
    "Nuri . . . . . ."
ADDRESS.
    "Khatpat Bazaar, Zanzibar"
PORT OF EMBARKATION.
    "Southampton, England"
PURPOSE OF VISIT TO KENYA.
    "In transit. On my way home to Zanzibar"
NATIONALITY.
    "British Protected Person"
RACE. *Race?*
    "Human"

I join the queue, form in hand, waiting to be interrogated. Fear in my belly, Grandma, the same fear you felt but never talked about. This white spirit is red-haired, but then you said they all looked alike to you, Grandma. A pukka sahib, in gleaming white shirt, khaki shorts, knee-length socks, polished brown shoes. I face him. "Smart Alec," he mumbles, reddening. Crosses out "Human,"

scribbles something in its place and motions me on to the gang-
way for "Disembarking Passengers, Customs to the Right."

Customs. A brown sahib, all of him in whites, shirt, shorts,
knee-length socks, leather shoes.

"Anything to declare?"

"No."

"London return Indian and nothing to declare?"

"I am here only for a few hours. On my way to Zanzibar."

"M.B.B.S.?"

"Beg your pardon?"

"M.B.B.S. – *M* for *miya*, husband. *B* for *bibi*, wife. And *B* and
S for *bacche saath*, with children," he laughs, turns his head and
spits out a mouthful of paan juice. "Joke, you see. Good, yes?"

I nod, smiling.

His eyes narrow on my camera.

"Let's see," he demands.

I comply.

"Ah, a box of Kodak," he sounds disappointed as he returns it.
"Leica is much better."

He looks at me again, hesitates, then waves me on. I feel his eyes
on my back, hear paan juice splash against the wall behind me.

⌘   ⌘   ⌘

"Nuri, weh Nuri. Nuriii, Noooorrriii." Mama Ayah, come to see
me.

"*Labek*, Mama," as I hurry down two flights of stairs, three
steps at a time. She is on the stool, Grandma's stool, draped in
soft *bui bui*, her face leathery lean. I go on my knees, facing her.

"*Mwanangu*," she cries, opening her arms to take me into the
folds of her *bui bui* musk. She pulls me back and squeezes my
cheek with her thumb and forefinger.

"But you have gone so thin, child. No meat on you. And so
pale, like a white man." She begins stroking my hair.

"They looked after me well, Mama."

"How about your meals?"

"My landlady cooked my meals. Not as good a cook as you, Mama, but she was caring."

She fidgets, then asks in a low voice, "A white woman?"

"Yes, Mama, a white woman."

"Eh?" She narrows her eyes, leans forward and asks in a murmur, "White man's truth?"

"Truth, Mama. God's Truth only," I say swishing my right hand under my chin. "Over there, white men work in coal mines, drive buses and work as porters, Mama."

"Hah," as she claps her hands. "Now I have heard everything."

"And there were black students, blacker than you. And brown students and students from as far away as China. And we were all the same in the white man's eyes."

She withdraws from her face, her eyes unseeing, fixed on the line of ants on the opposite wall. There is much I want to ask, but I must wait and watch as I did long ago under the mango tree.

"Your grandmother," she returns to herself, looking at me. "She told you to remember the things she taught you."

"How could I forget, Mama?"

"About the good and the evil."

"As with the spirits, Mama."

"About the real and the false."

"As with names, Mama."

"About the real you?"

"That the real me is within, Mama."

She nods a few times and then withdraws into herself again, still, silent.

⌘   ⌘   ⌘

Who, what is the real me? Born British Protected Person. Race Indian, 2nd class. Not white, 1st class, 1st division. Not Arab, 1st class, 2nd division. Not African. All blacks are African. They are natives. They have no class.

Zanzibar becomes independent. The new government passes a law. I cease being a British Protected Person. I am Zanzibari now.

Revolution. How many killed?

One, Hasnu the butcher.

Two, Huseini the teacher.

Three, Mzee Mohammed …

Ten? More like a hundred. A thousand. Ten thousand. Mass graves.

Zanzibar and Tanganyika form a union. They pass another law. I cease being Zanzibari. I am Tanzanian now, still 2nd class. Race Indian, capitalist, exploiter, bloodsucker. Not African. Not native. Natives have been abolished.

I emigrate. Fill in forms. Become a British Citizen. Part of the swamping black hordes come to sponge off the state. Race IndianPakiColouredBlack.

I emigrate again. To Calgary, Alberta. More forms. I am Canadian now. Of sorts. They call me Nick. Two false names. Doubly protected. Other Nicks here: Noormohamed, Nuruddin, Nashir, all Nicks.

Dastoor has become Dick.

And Sadruddin is Sam.

But Nuri persists, in the birth certificate, in passports, in school and distant university records, and throughout every changed nationality. Grandma knew. Nuri can come to no harm. He does not exist.

Halima

"What will you do when you are older?" Halima asks as we squat barefoot on the sand, our eyes on the crabhole that is as round as a ten-cent coin.

She asks hard questions. I do not reply.

"Run your grandfather's shop, I suppose," she says in the flat voice she uses when she is thinking.

"Uh-huh."

She picks a stick from the sand and holds it between her teeth.

"And you?" I ask.

"What?"

"What will you do?"

"Become an ayah in an Indian or Arab house."

I stare at her. She is pretty.

"Probably at someone like Sheikh Suleimani's," she mutters, sharp, through her teeth.

"Sheikh Suleimani?"

"Yesss," as she spits out the stick.

"The fat and –"

"Yes," she interrupts harshly, spits again, then turns to pick another stick.

"Marry me, Halima."

She tilts her head. "Silly, I am older than you." Her voice is now soft.

"You can help me look after Grandfather's shop. The way Grandma does."

"Besides." She turns to the crabhole and begins stirring it with the stick. The sand is hot, yielding. A crab darts out sideways.

"Aeiiii," she shrieks.

I dive for the crab and miss. Lying flat on the sand, I look up, see her raised leg, all the way up her long thigh. I look away at once. The ground shudders as her foot comes thumping down near the crab. She picks up the creature, struggling limbs in the air, puts it into the glass jar full of seawater. Our first catch of the day.

We sit down facing each other, legs stretched out on the sand. She is in her ankle-length *khanga* cloth. Her arms and shoulders bare, shiny smooth. She is taller than I am but I will catch up in a year or even sooner. Grandma says I am growing up fast. I can smell her, salt, fresh sweat, the blue and white washing soap Grandma allows her for bathing. She looks up, eyes squeezed against the sun. Dimples appear on each corner of her mouth when she speaks.

"What?" she asks as I watch her.

"You are pretty."

"I am black."

I continue looking at her as I level the sand near me. She chews on another stick, her teeth white and even.

"Mama Ayah is black and Grandma says she is my second mother."

"But she is only an ayah," she pouts.

"Grandma says we all grew up under her care. Father also. So she is both, mother and grandmother."

"An ayah is an ayah, Nuri. A servant."

She looks out into the sea and says, gently this time, "She is a good woman. Your grandma too. They help my mother even though she no longer works for your grandma. Yes, they are both good people. And they look after me and allow me to sleep at your place when my mother's away." She pauses, thinking, and then continues, "And sometimes even when she is not away."

"I like it when you sleep over at our house."

She looks up at me, grins. "I suppose when I am as old as your Mama Ayah, I too will be mother number two to someone like you."

She picks up the jar, looks closely at the crab, whispers, "But our elders always make decisions for us." Sometimes I do not understand why she speaks so seriously about the obvious.

I lie on the hot sand, close my eyes to the sun, feel the salt breeze on my face. She strokes the flat of my foot with a stick. I stay still. She moves on to the other foot. I jump up, grab her, throw her on her back but she is strong and is soon on top of me tickling me hard. I shout and laugh and struggle until she lets go. We throw ourselves down on our backs. I turn my head to look at her. She too is panting and her chest swells up bigger than Mother's. We start laughing again and roll ourselves over and over in the sand.

Mother does not mind my friendship with Halima, though she is strict about whom I go out with and when and where I go. She has all kinds of rules but I do not think she remembers them all. Some rules make sense and are good, like the one that allows me to eat as much as I want of whatever she cooks. No one is as good a cook as Mother. She sits on her low wooden stool in the kitchen, next to two open charcoal ovens, preparing meals for the whole house. "Mama, ghee," she orders. And Mama Ayah passes her ghee. "Mama, you peel the potatoes, I will do the *brinjal.*" And Mama Ayah brings in the pail of potatoes. And when I appear at the kitchen door, all Mother has to do is raise her eyes towards Mama Ayah and Mama Ayah gets up and gives me a cup of salty chicken soup or fingers out two fish eyes from the fried *changu.* Everyone knows fish eyes are for Nuri, and no one else gets them, not brother Sham, not sister Faiza. I roll each eye in my mouth first, suck in the tang of salt and curry, then gently press into its little softness with my front teeth until I reach the hard centre and then I bite it proper to make it as chewy as the *ubani* gum Grandma buys from Arab dhow merchants.

When it comes to chocolates, Mother's rules are very rigid and make no sense. When the shipment of chocolates comes in from England, mostly Nestlés, sometimes Cadbury's, I join Father and Hamisi at the godown which is not far from our house. The godown has no windows and is cool and dark and the only light comes through the open door. I wait near the crate marked in fat black ink "GULU IMPORTS, ZANZIBAR" beneath "CADBURY'S." Often the crate has the name of the ship, "*S. S. MODASA.*" Hamisi opens the crate, looks up for Father's nod, then takes out the first box for the house and gives it to me. English chocolates are hard, not like the gooey lumps Old Mama sells in the evenings in the square outside the old mosque. Hers are not really chocolates but little marble-size balls of jaggery. We point at the ones we want and if the price is agreed, five cents for the smaller and ten cents for the larger ones, she picks our choice with her long clean fingers and puts them in our palms. Her lumps do not contain nuts. English chocolates do. The whole round nut is best but the English are clever and sometimes put in only half nuts. I let my tongue lick the chocolate covering first. Then I bite into the nut, naked, woody. But Mother is strict about how many chocolate bars I can have.

"No more than one a day. Those are the rules."

"Just one more, pleeease," I beg.

She does not reply.

"I promise I won't eat one tomorrow."

She does not even look at me. Sometimes I think she pretends not to hear me. Continues with her knitting or fingering rice in the big round brass *thali* for little stones or combing her long black hair or pouting before the wall mirror for lipstick.

When Grandma is near, kneading millet dough for *rotlo*, she looks up and asks in a raised voice, "Why are you so strict with the child?"

"He had his share today."

"And what is wrong with the child having one more chocolate?"

"You will spoil him," Mother snaps.

"And what is wrong with a little spoiling?"

"Just wrong," Mother mumbles.

Grandma goes back to kneading her dough and says in a low voice, "Sometimes it is right to do wrong." Mother stares at Grandma, eyes as big as the whites of lychee. With Grandma on my side, I get my second chocolate but I do not feel the way I want to, like when I won a prize at school for reciting my favourite Gujarati poem about the disciple who disobeys his guru by staying on in a kingdom where everything – spinach, dates, furniture, cows, books, even gold – is valued the same. The silly disciple gets a pound of gold for a pound of his books. One day a thief enters the palace and steals the princess's necklace. The king orders the disciple to be hanged. But I am innocent, he cries. No matter, the king says. The real thief is too fat for the gallows and someone has to hang. You are thin enough. You will do.

I go to Mother as she sits down on the floor and try to give the chocolate back to her. She raises her chin, closes her eyes and looks away. I put my hand under her chin, turn her face towards me and try to push the chocolate into her bra where she keeps her ring of keys. She opens her hand to accept the chocolate, then hugs me tight. Mother smells different from Halima. Of *oudh* and imported Lux soap, except when she has just come out of the kitchen. Then she smells of masala. She opens the wrapper and gives me the first row of four pieces. I share two pieces with her and ask if we could keep one row for Halima and save the rest for tomorrow.

On one matter, Mother relaxes her strict rules. I am not allowed to go to the mosque at dawn because, she says, I need my sleep for growing up. But once or twice during holidays she takes me with her provided I have stayed out of trouble during the previous day. I often fall asleep in her lap as she sits cross-legged on the carpet saying her silent prayers. I sleep better there than at home, but the real reason I like going to the mosque in the mornings is our walk back. That is just before sunrise when darkness is about to leave Stone Town. The long empty lane feels narrower between rows of tall houses with their heavy wooden doors. No need to worry about evil spirits because we have just said our prayers and in any case Mother is with me. As we come to Kakoo the grocer's house, we hear him snore, loud as thunder. Samji the *khanga* merchant in the opposite house often snores back in reply. Mother and I laugh together, quietly. We do not talk. I keep my questions until we get home. Then I ask her if people who snore can dream at the same time or why the snoring does not wake them. Mother says early mornings are so peaceful. No one is about. The whole of Zanzibar is only for Mother and me, my hand in hers as we walk in silence. Except for the flip-flopping of our sandals. Last week we saw Sheikh Suleimani come out of Bi Leila's house, wiping his face with his long muslin *khanzu*. He looked to the left and then to the right and slunk away in the opposite direction. We were turning the corner then and I was about to say whom I had seen when Mother hurried us forward.

Grandma is different. She is not as strict as Mother and Mama Ayah says that she is deeply religious even though she rarely goes to the mosque.

"God is everywhere," she says to Mama Ayah, as they face each other sitting in the shop entrance in the evenings before Mother returns from her prayers and before Mama Ayah leaves for the night. "But mosques are for prayers," Mama Ayah insists.

"Huh," Grandma grunts. "As if Allah will not hear my prayers when I say them at home. These so-called sheikhs and scholars take us for fools, I tell you. They all speak from their asses, like your Sheikh Suleimani."

I giggle. Mama Ayah narrows her eyes in a stern look at me.

"Then why did you tell Sheikh Suleimani that his sermon on the Prophet's birthday was good?" Mama Ayah asks.

"In the first place, it was not a sermon. Just a long-winded speech given to the whole of Zanzibar in open grounds. In the second place, I did not say that his speech was good. The pompous fool asked me if I liked his speech and I said that I thoroughly enjoyed his performance."

"And what does that mean?" Mama Ayah asks.

"Exactly what I said. Have you not noticed how he starts the first word of every other sentence?"

Mama Ayah nods.

"With great effort, right?"

"Uh-huh."

"And his voice comes from deep down in his groin."

"So?"

"And at the same time he raises his right leg just that bit?" Grandma's thumb and index finger show a small gap. "As if the effort in pronouncing the first word is an effort to fart. Haiaiaiai."

Mama Ayah's face is long and serious. She looks at me, her frown forbidding me to laugh. I keep a straight face. She turns to Grandma, "What has that got to do with his speech?"

"That is what makes his speech entertaining, you silly woman. I am waiting for the day when the fool will actually let out that fart. Yaiyaiyaiyai."

Grandma is in tears as she smacks the flat of her hand hard on her thighs. I laugh out loud and Mama Ayah starts spluttering to hide her laughter.

Suddenly they stop laughing. "I know, I know, Mama," Grandma says in a low voice. "The less we talk about evil the better."

"And best not to have anything to do with him," Mama Ayah says, her face long and serious.

Grandma nods.

We sit still, look out into the empty lane, wait for Mother's return from the mosque.

With only one crab in Halima's glass jar, we walk by the low cemetery wall covered with lichen. I read aloud for Halima the names on the stones. "Moosa Yusuf, age 57, 10 June 1910. From Him we come. To Him we return." "Mariam binti Abdalla, age forty, 21 April 1901." I read the ones in Gujarati but not the ones in Arabic or English.

"I will teach you to read and write, Halima."

"What, Gujarati? I am not Indian."

"I will soon start learning English from Uncle Emarem and I can teach you as much as I am taught each day."

"What's the use? I can count, can't I? No one can cheat me. Just ask your grandma."

"But you can't read, Halima."

"Does your Mama Ayah read?"

I shake my head.

Halima's house is outside the town, past the cemetery and long past the English Club where white men play golf, all in whites: shirts, shorts, long socks and shoes. From a distance they look like crabs, walking one way and then another.

We come to a path through yellow, green and red bananas, none of them ripe yet. Halima's mother sells them outside the meat market. Red ones fetch a better price than the small yellow ones which in turn are more expensive than the long green ones. We enter a clearing, a mud and wattle hut with coconut leaf thatch, tall mangoes behind. Suddenly she stops, takes my hand into hers, presses it.

"What?" I ask.

"Shh."

We skirt round the clearing.

"I don't see anyone."

"Shhhh."

Sheikh Suleimani, tall with white and black beard, comes out of the hut. Shirt in hand, only a *shuka* round his waist, stomach big as the bagful of melons from Dodoma. Scratches his bald head under the cloth cap. He sees us, then looks around.

"Come, Halima, child, come," he calls.

Halima freezes.

He smiles through his yellow teeth, looks around again.

"So you are Nuri, Bi Zainabu's grandson."

His red eyes are close together, bulging out of his big face, so close that without the nose between them his two eyes would be one. I nod, holding on to Halima's hand. He dabs his face with the shirt. The soft fat on his face gives with each dab.

"Where is your mother?" he asks, looking at Halima.

Halima does not reply.

"She is not in there," he says, pointing towards the hut. "I suppose I will have to wait for her." He smiles his yellow smile again.

I feel the shudder in Halima's hand. Sheikh Suleimani turns round and walks towards the hut.

"Go, Nuri, go," Halima whispers, letting go of my hand.

Sheikh Suleimani sits in the wide rope seat in the shade of the hut.

"Yes, Nuri, you should go home now. It's late and your grandmother will worry about you. Halima and I will wait for her mother. Come, Halima."

I look at Halima. She gives me the glass jar, nods for me to go, walks towards him.

"Come and sit next to me, Halima. In the shade, it is cooler." He smiles as he wipes his face again with the shirt. Halima stretches her neck, gulps. The sheikh turns to me and says, "Did you not hear what I said? Go."

I start walking away, but turn round when I hear Halima sob. He shushes her, his left hand under her chin, his right hand stroking her bare arm. He sees me, barks, "*Go*, I say, go *now*."

Halima pulls herself free from him, runs towards the mangoes in the back. The roaring monster is now running towards me, his two eyes as one, shaking his fist at me. I fling the glass jar and it hits him in the face. "Ya Allah," he cries. I turn round and run.

I run all the way home, up the stairs, three steps at a time, to the front room where Grandma is drying her hands on a towel.

"I have killed him, Grandma," I cry, hands on forehead.

Grandma drops the towel, rushes towards me. "What happened, my child?" She squats on the floor, takes my face into her hands, wipes tears from my eyes with each of her thumbs. "Tell me, child, what happened."

"I have killed him, Grandma. He was running towards me, threatening like …"

"Who, my child?"

"Threw the jar at him and he cried and, and …"

She presses me deep into her chest. "Where were you?"

"At Suleimani's," I sob. "No, at Halima's and Suleimani came running to catch me and…"

She sits down on the linoleum floor, takes me into her lap. I cling to her, face pressed into her yielding sandalwood scented belly. She feels my head and murmurs, "Fever."

I jerk out of her lap, shake her by her shoulders and shout, "Why won't you listen, Grandma? I have killed Sheikh Suleimani."

Mother rushes into the room and I run towards her. She takes me into her lap. My back rests on her chest, her arms clasped round me, my hands clutching her arms. She strokes my hair and asks in a soft voice, "What did Grandma tell you to do when you have difficulties?"

I look at Grandma who begins to recite the Prophet's Call-to-Ali prayer. Mother and I join her. We recite it three times. Grandma says that is the best number because the prayer ends in the three calls to Ali.

Mother rocks and begins the drone of a prayer she often sings in the mornings in the mosque.

> *He has no name nor abode*
> *Nor is He without name or abode*
> *Call on Him by any name*
> *The Nameless One with a million names*

"Sheikh Suleimani is not easy to kill," I hear Grandma say.

I look at her.

"Because the police would have come to our house long before now."

In the morning I hide myself round the corner from Sheikh Suleimani's house and wait. He comes out alive, with no bandage round his head. I whisper my *shukr*, thank you, to Ali. Master Raval gives me only detention after school for being late. I say another *shukr* to Ali.

At night I join Grandma and Mama Ayah in the shop entrance. Grandfather has gone to sleep and I stretch myself on his long seat, waiting for Mother to return from the mosque.

Halima has not come to the house for three days. Grandma has not complained as she does even when Halima is only a few minutes late in the morning to run her errands. Every time I ask Grandma and Mama Ayah about Halima, they look into my eyes as if they suspect I know the answer, and then reply, "She has not shown up." They are hiding something from me but do not know they are not at all good at doing so. Halima cannot be ill. Of that I am sure because Grandma would have sent me with Mama Ayah to see her as she did last year. I hear them talk in whispers.

"And her mother, Mama?"

"Yes, yes, she approves," whispers Mama Ayah.

I keep my eyes shut, pretending to sleep. They begin talking about a man, how old he is and what work he does. I do not get all they say except when Mama Ayah sighs and says that she was much younger when she got married. I think of what Halima said. That an ayah is an ayah. That she is older than I am. That important decisions are always made by our elders. I am not sure if Halima's mother and Grandma and Mama Ayah have made decisions about Halima. Have they sent her away, as protection from the sheikh? Or married her off?

I know it is impolite to interrupt grown-up talk but I jump out of the long seat and shout, "What have you done with Halima, Grandma?"

Grandma and Mama Ayah stare at me.

"Why have you been so mean to her?"

They look at each other.

"I know she is older than I am but Amina Aunty is older than Hasan Uncle and they have two children."

"Come, child," Grandma opens her arms for me.

"No, Grandma. Tell me about Halima first."

Mother returns from the mosque.

"Why will you not allow Halima to come and live with us so that she is safe from Suleimani, Mother? Why can't I marry her? I will teach her to read, write and, and …" I am sobbing.

Mother comes towards me, says that such important matters are best discussed in the morning after a good night's rest. I shrug my shoulders, rub tears off my cheeks. She takes a chocolate bar from her purse and holds it out for me. I push it away. "I don't want it," I shout. She takes me into her *halood* side, presses me hard, strokes my hair.

The Squint

"I am worried," Grandma's voice, from her own bed, floats across the room towards Grandfather's.

She begins the night in my bed by the centre window. When she decides I am asleep she removes my arm clinging round her waist and my leg from across her long lean thigh. She then whispers Ali prayers over me and tiptoes to her own bed by the left window. Best of all is when she is sure I am asleep and starts talking to Grandfather from my bed. I keep my eyes shut tight and feel her squashy belly begin to firm and then rise to push the words inside her to her paan-filled mouth.

"Nuri's grandfather," is how she starts, except when she is worried. She never gets a reply the first time so she waits before calling again. Sometimes she calls him "Gulu's father," but Gulu is not Father's real name, as Nuri is not my real name either. Grandma insists we use our false names to confuse evil spirits.

Some nights she does not go to her own bed but slinks off to Grandfather's by the right window. Then their words are not so easy to catch because they talk in whispers, which get mixed up with the squeaks in Grandfather's bed. In the mornings Grandfather bends down to look at the springs under the bed and mumbles "*sala*," "*harami*" and other forbidden words.

"I said I am worried," Grandma's voice comes again from her bed.

Grandfather clears his throat. He *nkhuus* even during daytime to let her know he is awake or listening or just that her words have reached his good ear.

"I am worried about our Nuri," Grandma again.

"What has he done?"

"Nothing. He is barely ten. I am worried about his innocence."

Or did she say, "I am worried, he is innocent"? I do not know why she thinks I am innocent because one night I heard her tell Grandfather that Khan the fez cap merchant saw me jump off his roof, two storeys up. Khan's roof is only one storey high but everyone knows Grandma is short and she exaggerates. Grandfather sighed his "Hai, hai," and asked Allah to "instill some sense in the child." I pretended I was asleep.

"He's done nothing, you say?"

"No, nothing."

A pause. They have many pauses. Grandma says pauses are full of sleep and Grandfather often falls into them.

"And he is innocent, you say?"

"Yes."

"Huh, huh, woman, and you say you are *worried*?"

"If that is the way you feel, then my tongue shall go silent."

I wonder if Grandma will refuse to speak. Mama Ayah says Grandma went on a speech strike once. She did not talk to Grandfather for a whole month. Something to do with Bi Mongi, Mama Ayah thinks, but nobody else remembers why. The only day in the year Grandma does not talk is the one day in the month of Ramadhan when she fasts. That day ends in the Night of Power which is the holiest of all the holy nights because on that night the Prophet received the first of Allah's revelations. The whole of that day Grandma spends in bed with a headache.

"Gulu's mother, if it is about the child Nuri that you are worried, then you must tell me."

"I meant the Squint," says Grandma.

"Who?"

"Don't who, who me."

"So you still have that bee buzzing in your head?" Grandfather cries, but not loudly, as if spitting his words through his false teeth. He must have forgotten to remove them before going to bed.

Grandma does not reply, not even to remind him about his teeth. I suppose she knows that one does not argue with Grandfather when he is angry. She also knows that he is never annoyed for long. That is because he is very old and has a short memory.

"Gulu's mother," Grandfather says at last, his voice no longer harsh. "What worries you worries me too. You know that."

"I told you. It is the Squint."

Squint is Grandma's name for Bi Mongi. Grandma insists she has seen Bi Mongi's squint and that the reason we have not noticed it is Bi Mongi's cunning, the way she lowers her eyes when she speaks so as to hide her squint, and also to look more attractive, more humble than she really is. "God has a sense of humour," she huffs. "Allowing her to be named Mongi, Expensive, when there is not a bone in her that is not cheap."

"But Nuri gets on well with her, doesn't he?" Grandfather asks.

"Gets on well with her, indeed."

"And Juma is always with him when he visits Bi Mongi?"

"Juma indeed. Juma ought to know better. Tch. Poor Juma."

"Fret not, Gulu's mother," Grandfather says, his voice gentle. "The child will come to no harm."

Grandma has many worries, mostly about the family. About our servant Hamisi, if his sudden loss of weight may be the result of an illness they have not found a name for. About Leli Aunty who has gone on a Gandhi fast. "A woman ought to be big enough for the husband she will one day marry, and for the strong babies she will have to carry and I will not allow any daughter of mine to slim herself out of marriage." About Father because, though he takes his crumpled cotton jacket from under the mattress and his brown tasselled fez cap off the hook for prayers, he does not go to the mosque but instead goes to play cards with his friends at the club near the sea front. Grandma worries even when she cannot raise a belch after a meal because that means she has not thanked

Allah. Mama Ayah says that Grandma is full of love for us and that is part of the cause of her worry, though I can never get her to tell what the rest of the cause of Grandma's worry may be.

Bi Mongi is certainly different, different from Grandma, different from anyone I know. Her long hair is red in the sun and black in the dark. "Clever henna colouring," Grandma snaps. And Bi Mongi's eyes are *bhoori bhoori* brown. "Crafty, hiding her squint," Grandma says. Bi Mongi's skin has no wrinkles, no marks, is smooth across her round face and along her arms down to her narrow feet and hennaed toenails. "Half-Indian, half-Arab mongrel," Grandma snorts. Grandma's skin changes to roasted almond brown in hot season but Bi Mongi's never loses its pale smooth shine. "Hasn't done a day's work in her life," Grandma explains. "And all the fortune she spends on the perfumes she buys from the Muscat dhow merchants." Whenever she grumbles about Bi Mongi, she ends up with a sigh for her poor Juma. She thinks Bi Mongi does not treat him well. He sweeps floors and runs errands for Bi Mongi and all he gets in return are leftovers.

Juma is the tallest man in the whole of Zanzibar, taller than Grandfather. And he is strong, the strongest man in the world, stronger than even Charles Atlas. Charles Atlas cannot lift the bale of *khanga* cloth the way Juma does. His legs apart, feet bare, he sinks a steel hook into the bale with one hand and tilts it towards him. His mouth opens just enough to show the whitest teeth I have ever seen. A slight jerky squat, a mighty "Ya Allah," and he heaves the bale up onto his back. His eyes open wide into a red stare as he steadies himself on his feet. His biceps bulge into balloons. Passers-by stop to watch. Kakoo the grocer and his customers come out into the lane. Khan the fez cap merchant adjusts his cap, leaves his press and stands on his stone step to look. All the sewing machines at Bhikhoo the tailor's grow silent. Grandfather sits up on his bench. Grandma starts murmuring her prayers, eyes closed, calling on Ali, the Friend of Allah, the Revealer of Wonders.

Bent with the bale on his back, Juma thumps one heavy step after another towards the last unlit room on the ground floor. All is silence until we hear his *oomph* from deep inside the shop and then we know all is well. Grandma's prayers end when Juma reappears, still slightly bent. She asks him to sit on the stone step and wait for the coffee vendor to pass by. Grandfather goes back to sleep in his chair. Khan strokes his moustache, adjusts his cap again and returns to his press. Kakoo and his customers disappear into his store, and Bhikhoo's sewing machines start whirring again.

Juma is Bi Mongi's servant, but he works for anyone who pays him, and sometimes for nothing at all just because he feels like it. Everyone wants him to work for them, but Juma says, "I am no one's servant except Juma's." He is often at Bi Mongi's, dozing on the stone step to her entrance. At night he spreads himself across the entrance as a night watchman. No thief dare cross the Charles Atlas of Zanzibar. Bi Mongi hardly talks to him. She hardly talks to me either. And she never calls me by my name and never asks if Grandma and Grandfather are well, which she should even if she does not mean it.

Juma is a wizard with a football. Once he has the ball, nobody can get it without fouling him. He once played for Zanzibar in the Gossage Cup match against Kenya. He never refuses to make up the team when we are short of players, or to referee our games. He likes all my friends, though I think I am his favourite. Grandfather likes Juma because, he says, Juma is a genuine person. When I ask him to explain, he says that Juma is happy being himself and does not feel the need to impress others. Grandfather also thinks that as long as Juma is around, we are all safe. Bi Mongi is not at all like Juma. Sometimes I think she resents children. I often wonder how Juma got her to agree to allow me to visit him at her house on Saturday afternoons. We meet on the third floor, which has old English newspapers, mostly the *Times*, piled up against one wall. Juma says that the house once belonged to Bi Mongi's brother who collected old English newspapers from the English Club for a small payment and planned to read them one day in order to understand how the English think. But words are often used to hide meanings and thoughts, Juma says and laughs. The only way to tell what the English think is to look at what they do. In any case, Bi Mongi's brother died before he could read the papers and Bi Mongi, who inherited the house, never got rid of them. Just as well the English newspapers are on the third floor which is never used by Bi Mongi because, she says, it is directly under the corrugated iron roof and therefore too hot for her. The only advantage of having a third floor, she thinks, is to keep the heat off the second floor where she does her cooking, eating and sleeping. Juma shows me how to make paper boats, a fisherman's canoe, a two-funnel steam ship and, most difficult of all, a dhow with a sail. The English newspaper, the *Times*, is larger in size than our own Sunday editions of *Zanzibar Voice* or *Samachar* so that our paper boats are larger than anyone else's in the whole of Stone Town. We store our best boats at Bi Mongi's until the rains come, when the lane becomes a river for them to sail on, up to Kakoo the grocer's gutter round the corner.

Sometimes Bi Mongi comes to the third floor when Juma and I are busy with our boats, her thin *khanga* cloth wrapped round her from chest to ankles, her arms and shoulders bare, her hair wavy long with jasmine flowers tied at the back. Never a greeting from her for either of us. She sits on the floor by the wall, her big eyes lowered, her elbows resting on raised knees. Every now and then she looks up. When Juma looks back at her, she smiles. I too get one of her smiles when I am caught watching her, but she does not know that I am looking for the squint. Juma never makes mistakes folding paper boats when we are on our own, but he does when Bi Mongi is with us. I am certain she makes him nervous. Maybe that is why Grandma does not like her. Sometimes she stretches her bare arm and presses her hand gently on his, and Juma gurgles. Once she undid a little of her *khanga* cloth to wipe off sweat beads on Juma's face, cooing softly, "My tamarind muscle man." I looked away to avoid seeing the silly grin on Juma's lowered head.

I cannot ask Grandma what Bi Mongi has to do with her worry about me because then she will know I was only pretending to be asleep when she talked to Grandfather from her bed. I should ask Mama Ayah. She has been our ayah since before Father was born and knows more about Grandma than even Mother. She is a walking library and much easier to get information from than the sour-faced Janu the librarian in Kiponda Street. She is an all-rounder who can mix turmeric and the whites of an egg to apply to a sprained ankle or mix spices with honey in boiled milk for colds. And no one knows more about spirits.

"But if some evil spirits come in human form, how can you tell?" I ask Mama Ayah by the water tap in the kitchen as she chews on her *mswaki* twig she uses for brushing her teeth. She brushes her teeth twice a day, once after breakfast, which she has on her own when we have all finished ours, and once at the end of the day when her work is done. She thinks Grandma has no teeth because Grandma never brushes, but Grandma says she does not brush because she has no teeth. "In any case," Grandma says, "the important thing is to keep one's mouth clean for saying Allah's name."

"What?" Mama Ayah mumbles through her teeth.

"But how can you see an evil spirit?" I ask her. "How can you tell if it is an evil spirit?"

She turns towards me and mumbles again, "The way you catch grasshoppers. You concentrate."

"On what, Mama?"

"The evil spirit's feet. They face the wrong way." She lowers her face close to mine and whispers, all serious, "Why do you want to know?"

Her eyes are deep into mine and I cannot look away. I think she knows I will not tell her the whole story. Her lips pressed onto the *mswaki*, she beams, then slides her hard dry hand under my chin.

"Tell me, *mwanangu*," she says in a gentle voice as she raises my chin, the *mswaki* pushed to the side of her mouth, her eyes

still into mine. She calls me *mwanangu*, my child, when she wants
me to do or tell her something or just because she is pleased with
me.

"If an evil spirit has something wrong with her," I begin.

"Or *him*," she corrects me.

"Like having her feet pointing the wrong way."

"Or *his* feet pointing the wrong way."

"Or having a squint?"

"Aha."

She holds me by my shoulders and says, "Listen to me,
mwanangu. As long as you have your Grandmother, and that is for
always, you have nothing to worry about."

The best time to ask Grandma about anything important is when
she is threading beads on the low stool in the entrance to our shop,
usually early in the morning. She sells threaded glass beads to out-
of-town villagers. She starts with a high asking price, which is re-
jected at once by the customer who, after some hesitation, suggests
a much lower price. Grandma's eyes light up, then close as she
pretends to consider the buyer's offer. Forefinger on her lower lip,
she shakes her head and suggests another price. Backwards and
forwards they go and only for a few cents. If the customer decides
not to make a purchase and leave, Grandma relents by suggesting
a yet lower price and the haggle starts all over again. If the street
coffee vendor is about with his conical brass pot on a charcoal pan,
she asks the customer to join her in the little cup of thick black
coffee and then the conversation turns to the price of mangoes or
eggs or the late rains.

Grandma is in her heavy velvet frock, her head-cover round her
shoulders. She never covers her head, not even for Grandfather,
except in the presence of very old men who come to visit Grandfather. I sit cross-legged on the floor facing her and, after a pause,
ask, "How do people get squints, Grandma?"

She looks down at me, then goes back to her beads. She has
difficulty with a red bead, wets the thread end with the paan juice

in her mouth, narrows her eyes. Her forehead wrinkles deepen in concentration. When the thread gets through the bead, she turns to me and says, "When a woman is pregnant and she looks at the moon for long periods she gives birth to a child with a squint." Her eyes are into mine the way Mama Ayah's were when I asked her about evil spirits having squints. "Or it happens when a pregnant woman sees a person with a squint."

She goes back to her beads and then, without looking at me, asks, "Have you been talking to Mama Ayah?"

I should have known she would suss out what I have been up to. I do not reply. She looks at me again, puts down her bead basket, stretches her arms for me to get into. She presses me deep into her side.

"Mama Ayah is superstitious," she says as she strokes my hair. "You have nothing to worry about. You have a false name that protects you. And you have the *vigani* charm you wear on your right arm. Very potent. I paid a whole shilling to the *mwalimu* to blow his most powerful prayers on it."

Suddenly, I want to ask her why she told Grandfather she is worried. But I decide not to because if she feels I am well protected, Bi Mongi is probably not the real reason. Not her squint anyway. Maybe something to do with what Grandfather did, something naughtier than forgetting or pretending to forget to slide in his false teeth when he goes out or buying cheap fatty goat meat. Maybe Mama Ayah is right, that Grandma loves us all and, in any case, it is in the nature of all grandmothers to worry.

Juma greets me with a scowl. Maybe he is tired or had an argument with someone, perhaps with Bi Mongi. I can never tell with the grown-ups. He makes the first fold in the large sheet on the floor.

"Why don't we make a boat big enough for us to sit in, Juma?"

"What, Nuri?"

"You are not listening, Juma. Why can't we make a boat big enough to sit in?"

His scowl is now a half-smile. "There is no paper big or strong enough for that," he says, but his heart is not in his words.

"Father gets many cardboard boxes from England and Japan."

Juma completes the second fold.

"And I could get the glue from Khan," I continue. "The glue he makes for his fez caps is the best."

"Let me give it a think," he says.

Suddenly he becomes still, as if listening. I smell vapours from scented sticks burning in Bi Mongi's censer. And then we hear a soft cry from the second floor, "Juuuumaaa."

"I am needed," he says. "We will finish tomorrow."

"You will let me know soon, Juma? About the glue?"

He stands up and goes to the stairs. He waits for me to pass. I run all the way to Khan's shop.

"Salaam, Khan Saheb."

Khan is in his cane chair facing the collapsible counter on which are three red fez caps and some tassels. He is a large man with a neat beard trimmed to look like the end of the hairy shell of a coconut and his eyes are set deep into his face under shaggy brows. He returns my salaams without looking at me as he is busy fixing a tassel on the flat top of the cap he has in hand. I sit on the counter and watch him.

"There," he grins, raising the fez cap with its broad leather band inside.

"This is a special one," he says.

"Such a big head, Khan Saheb?"

"You can say that," he smiles, then adds, "As big as it is thick."

We laugh together. I do not ask him whose head. One does not ask shopkeepers about their customers. He waves me towards him and allows me to feel the fez.

"My father came from Peshawar, you know," he says softly, looks at me, and continues, "He taught me all I know."

I like Khan and the way he presses the soft fez into the steel mould on the press board. He grabs the handles of the steaming upper cover and brings it down to close onto the lower mould, just long enough for the hissing cover to stiffen the fez into a bright red cap. Then comes the best part: we inhale the steamy smell of the heated fez.

Before I can ask him where Peshawar is, he asks, "Why are you not playing this afternoon, Nuri?"

"Juma is busy."

"Huhn," he grunts as I pass him a fez cap from the counter board.

"But Juma has agreed to make a big boat for me." He turns the fez round in his hand.

"Juma is a man of many talents, Nuri."

"Yes, big enough for me to sit in."

Khan looks at me, smiles as I hand him a tassel from the counter board.

"But we will need something good and strong to hold it together, Khan Saheb."

"That you will, Nuri."

"And I told him you make the best fez caps in Zanzibar and the best glue."

"You are right on the first count, Nuri, since I am the only one in the town who makes fez caps, and I also agree with you about the glue."

I look at his press table where he keeps the glue.

"It is on the lower shelf," he says, without looking at me.

I go to the press table. The tin bowl on the lower shelf is half full with creamy green paste.

"How much do you sell it for, Khan Saheb?"

"I sell fez caps, Nuri."

I look at the tin bowl again. "Not much left, Khan Saheb."

"Half full the last time I saw it."

I stare at the glue. "But it looks stale."

He roars with laughter and asks, "How much will you need for your big boat, Nuri?"

I look at the bowl again.

"Will what is there be enough?" he asks.

"Oh yes, Khan Saheb."

"Then take it, Nuri."

I turn to look at him. He is busy with the tassel.

"But how much –"

"There is no charge between friends."

"Can I take it now, Khan Saheb?"

He nods.

As I leave the shop, I lower my eyes and say, "I will not jump off your roof again, Khan Saheb."

He looks at me and says, "Not off any roof. Promise?"

I nod. He smiles, waves me out, saying, "Use it soon, else it will dry up."

I run all the way back to Bi Mongi's. Juma should still be there. Bi Mongi is not in the entrance. Nor is Juma. The door is open but no one answers my *hodi*. I repeat my request for permission to enter, *hodi*, *hodi*, louder this time. No cry of *karibu*, welcome. I enter and go up the first staircase, which opens into Bi Mongi's bedroom, the coolest room in the house because the sun does not reach it. She is asleep in bed by the far wall. I walk quietly towards the staircase to the third floor. The large sheets of paper are near the verandah where Juma left them. I leave the glue bowl in the cool of the shade in the corner. No sense waiting. I go down the steep stairs to the second floor and look at Bi Mongi again. Her long hair falls over the side of the bed and curls down to the floor. I want to touch it. I tiptoe over to her bed. Her perfume smells sweaty. As I stretch out my hand, I see Juma, covered by the bed sheet, except for his face, which is buried in her neck and his long black arm slung round her white, white chest. Bi Mongi is on her side, right thigh bare. I jerk back. She opens her big eyes on me. I run for the stairs. Grandma is right. In the left eye. The squint.

I do not know what to do. I must see Juma, but what will I say to him? I could start by telling him that I have come to remind him to use the glue before it dries up.

"*Hodi, hodi.*"

"*Karibu*, welcome," I hear Bi Mongi from inside the entrance.

I greet her, go past her towards the stairs.

"Come, my child," I hear her call. I stop. "Come," she calls again. I turn round and start going back to her.

"I am sorry, Bi Mongi."

She looks up, smiles. "It is all right, *mwanangu*," she says, waves me closer to her, starts stroking my hair. "I thought we frightened you, Nuri child."

She is gentle. She smells of the sweet perfume from the scented sticks she burns in her censer.

"Juma is not in, Nuri child."

"But he must use the glue before it dries up."

"That is important, I know. Don't worry. I will tell him."

Should I tell Grandma that she was right all along about Bi Mongi's squint? How will she feel if I do? She will certainly start with her "hows" and "whens" and "whys" and may get even more angry with Grandfather. Whatever happened was probably between Grandfather and Bi Mongi, so Grandma could not be angry with Juma. And Bi Mongi called me *mwanangu* and then also by my name. Maybe I was wrong about her. She is kinder than I thought. But she likes Juma, and as Juma is my friend, she will not want to upset him and he will not let her harm me. In any case, I am well protected. Grandma said so herself. So did Mama Ayah. Maybe I should wait. I will soon be grown up and then Grandma's worries will be over.

A Little Unwellness

Grandfather comes to my bed by the centre window, hairy chest bare, *khanga* cloth round his waist. He lifts the mosquito net, feels my forehead.

"Hmmm. A slight fever." He lets the mosquito net down, stands still, shaven head white in the early morning sun. "You are not to go to school today, Nuri child," he says, looking down at me through the mosquito net. And then, as if nothing is the matter, he walks slowly to the rocking chair by the door for his prayers.

His prayer is in Kutchi, not at all like the set prayer the rest of us have to learn. Starting with *"Bismillah* ... In the name of Allah ..." we have to chant right through to *"Ash haado aan* ... I bear witness ..." Grandfather's is more like talk, only he calls it prayer. He goes through the names of everyone at home and of all uncles and aunts and cousins who live on the mainland. Eighteen names and never in the same order. On school days, I lie in until he comes to my name, then I jump out of bed, walk slowly past him and run down the stairs to the second floor to brush my teeth and wash my face by the tap in the kitchen. I get into my school uniform and have to present myself before Mother for inspection. No matter how careful I am, she always finds some place along my waist to tuck my white shirt into the blue shorts. And then the worst part. She grabs my face with her left hand to comb my "thick and unruly" hair. I stand still, eyes shut tight. Any squirming, wiggling or screeching turns her grip into a crusher.

I can stay on in bed today and listen to the whole of Grandfather's prayer. Grandfather says he can tell I am not well even before he feels my forehead for fever because when I am ill I babble in my sleep. When he has a worry, he begins, eyes shut, with a special request, as he does this morning.

> *O Lord, accept first the two requests of this Your slave. One is on behalf of Your slave Nuri who is not well. Look after him, my Lord, and make him well soon. The second request, O Lord, concerns Your slave Hamisi, our servant. Something is wrong with him and, stubborn that he is, he says nothing about it. Now, Lord, you know this worries another of Your slaves, Nuri's grandmother, and what worries her worries me too. That is why, O my Lord and Master, I beseech you to cure Your slave Hamisi of whatever it is that ails him or at least cure Your slave Nuri's grandmother of her worry. But if it is Your will that neither should happen, then I pray for strength to see us through.*

Everybody else is worried about Hamisi too. Nobody knows what is wrong with him. His face is a swollen scowl. Nothing is left of his smile. Nor of the shine in his eyes. Even his breathing out during afternoon sleep is a long *aaaaa* instead of a gentle *soooo*.

Grandfather opens his eyes to begin his regular prayer of names. I get out of bed. He turns to look at me. My head feels light as I walk towards him. On holidays I often sit down cross-legged on the floor next to his rocking chair. He never minds my doing so as long as I keep quiet and have my palms open and raised for Allah's Grace until his prayer is over. Today he holds out his arms for me, lifts me into his lap and begins his list of names. He starts with, "Your slave Nuri's grandmother, Your slave Gulu, Your slave

Sham," and goes all the way through to, "Your slave Ayah and Your slave Hamisi."

Grandfather never uses our real names but that is because he is either too old to remember them or he does not want evil spirits to hear them. In any case, Allah knows our real names.

When he thinks he has mentioned all eighteen names, he pauses and clears his throat, which is a sign for me to tell him if he has omitted anyone. If he has left out a name, I mention it in a low voice and he asks the Lord to include it in his list. Most times, though, he is good. He has not forgotten anyone's name today so I nod for him to go on, but instead of starting on the last part of his prayer, he says, "You have been wandering, child. I have not mentioned your name yet." He feels my forehead and, holding me close, starts again with, "O Lord, look after this little slave of Yours, a favourite of mine, as You did Hasan and Hussein, grandsons of Your Prophet, on whom may You always shower Your blessings."

He takes my hands into his and raises them for the last part of his prayer. Eyes shut and head moving from side to side, he lowers his voice to a whisper.

> *O my Lord and Master, we are full of faults, as you well know. And undeserving slaves that we all are, I beg for forgiveness of our sins. Give us our bread, O Lord, and be kind to us. Have mercy upon us, Ya Allah, and keep us on the straight path always, always, Amen.*

After the prayers, he enters the washroom. The tap brings fresh water from a narrow pipe, which runs by the two walls of the open verandah. In the afternoons the pipe gets very hot, and the water even hotter. But in early mornings, when Grandfather has his quick sit under the tap, it is "ho ho ho aa aa Yaa Aallaah" cold. He never uses soap. That is why, Grandma says, his skin has a creamy feel. And then he starts going down the stairs, right foot on the first step, calling, "Ya Ali" or "Ya Hussein" or one of the other three holy names, followed by the left foot. When both feet

are together again, he starts all over, with the right foot and "Ya
Fatima" or "Ya Hasan." Everyone in the house knows when
Grandfather begins his descent. Mama Ayah goes to the kitchen
to get his early morning chai left brewing on the charcoal fire by
Grandma. Hamisi waits for Grandfather at the end of the staircase to help him to a chair by the table. Today I go down the stairs
before Grandfather comes out of the washroom, sit on the chair
by the table, arms crossed against my chest. He takes his time
coming down and, once seated, Hamisi sits on the last step of the
staircase, facing Grandfather. Grandfather pours chai from the
cup into the saucer and slides the bottom of the cup across the
saucer rim for the drips. He looks at Hamisi and begins, as always,
with, "Are you well, Hamisi?"

"Yes, I am well, Old Father," is Hamisi's usual reply, but today
he adds, "except for this little unwellness that is within me."

"What is it, Hamisi?"

Hamisi looks down at his feet and does not reply.

"So you are still not better, eh, Hamisi?"

Grandfather lifts the saucer to his mouth, raises his eyes to
look at Hamisi again, then empties the saucer in two loud slurps.
He pours the rest of the chai into the saucer, lowers his head to
blow on it, raises the saucer and this time slurps it all down in one
gulp. He looks at Hamisi, waves the empty cup towards me and
says, "Nuri is not well today either. But his illness, *Inshallah*, Allah
willing, should pass in a day or two. Yours is clearly more serious."

Hamisi, who continues staring at his feet, says nothing.
Grandfather turns towards me, stretches to feel my forehead, and
says, "And you, child, you are not to go out today." He looks at
Hamisi again, shakes his head and gets up with a "Ya Allah" to go
to the stairs leading to the ground floor where Grandma has
already opened the store. I follow him. He is slow. I squeeze past
him on the staircase and he interrupts his call to the Holy Ones
with an annoyed "*ah, ha, ho.*"

Grandma is on her low stool by the entrance threading her beads. She puts down her basket and waves me to her, "You look flushed, *beta*. Come, *beta*, come."

I feel faint as I walk towards her. She feels my forehead first, then my cheeks, a frown on her face. "A slight temperature, *beta*. You must rest today."

Grandfather comes and sits on the long wooden bench facing Grandma. He stares at me, then stretches his arms for me to get into. I put my head on his lap and stretch myself on the bench. I wish I could spend the whole day on the ground floor but I know Grandma will not allow it and will soon send me off to my bed on the third floor to get well for school tomorrow.

"Have you got the note to your teacher, Nuri child?" Grandfather asks, his hand on my forehead.

"Un-hum."

I keep Grandfather's note to Master Rathod in a safe place, in the fold of the cover of the book of tables. This way I always have it ready to give to the master on my return to school after illness. We call Master Rathod Sprinkler Rathod. That is because he has false teeth and hisses out sprays. I am glad he never reads Grandfather's note aloud. It looks like one long word:

letthemasterjibeinformedthatmygrandsonnuriwasnotwell yesterdayandcouldnotcometoschoolsopleaseexcusehisabsence.

Nobody can read Grandfather's handwriting. Grandma says that once he has written something, he cannot read it back himself. She is convinced my Master Rathod cannot read it either. When Sprinkler Rathod opens the note, his eyes narrow. He lifts his glasses slowly to his forehead and brings the note closer to his eyes. When the note touches his long eyelashes, he gives a shudder, lets his glasses drop on his nose and returns it with a muffled "*umph*." Grandfather's note has no date and can be used again and again until I lose it and then I have to ask him for a new note. No use asking Father because he always says he is busy and he dates his notes so I can use them only once.

"I shall give him *faki* powder before his breakfast. He should be well in a day," says Grandma.

"Allah willing," says Grandfather.

"*Inshallah*," repeats Grandma.

The worst of being unwell is to have to drink down *faki* mixed with chai. Grandma and Mama Ayah mix ten stinky powders: some black, some green, one brown and one yellow. I have to hold my nose and drink it down in large gulps. If anyone in the house shows the slightest sign of illness, Grandma is on to them with her *faki*. She says it cleans the system and is good for colds, coughs, fevers, tummy upsets and other sicknesses I have not yet caught. Three long visits to the lavatory can cure anyone of anything, I guess.

Hamisi comes in and sits next to Grandfather on the floor, facing Grandma. When Hamisi is not well, nobody asks him to do anything and Father has to do his work, cycling to the post office or to the Clove Growers' building or to Customs for licences to order goods from other countries.

"Hamisi is still unwell," says Grandma without looking up from her beads. "He's hardly eaten anything these three days."

I look at Hamisi but his eyes are either closed or he is looking down at his feet. He says nothing. I look at Grandfather. His open eyes are unblinking and fixed on nothing.

"I said Hamisi is not better yet," Grandma repeats, louder. I look again at Hamisi and Grandfather, but both are still.

"Grandfather's good ear has not caught your words, Grandma," I say, but without laughing.

Hamisi once told me that Grandfather is old and therefore deaf but only in one ear and that nobody knows, not even Grandfather, which ear is the good one.

Grandma looks up and says, "Don't you believe that nonsense about one good ear, *beta*. He can hear everything." She looks down again and adds, "When he wants to."

Grandma is right. Sometimes Grandfather can hear a whisper. In any case, it is best not to say anything in his presence if he is not meant to hear it. I wish I were old. Then I would answer only those questions I chose to, no matter who asks.

"*Khuuuu*," Grandfather clears his throat. Hand still on my forehead, he says, "I got deaf having to listen all my life to your grandma talk." We both laugh. So does Hamisi, his first one in many days. Grandma looks up at him and her face relaxes into a grin.

"And now, Hamisi," Grandfather begins, "listen to what I have to say. Nuri's grandmother has always treated you well, has she not?"

Hamisi, still looking at his feet, nods.

"So now I speak not as your employer but as your elder. Do you understand?"

Hamisi looks up. "Yes, Old Father," he says.

"We know you have not been well these few days. But you have not seen fit to talk to anyone about it, not even to Nuri's grandmother."

"I am sorry, Old Father."

"In that case, tell us now what is the matter with you."

"It is my tooth," Hamisi whimpers after a pause. He winces as he raises his hand to his right jaw.

"Must be really bad, Hamisi, this toothache, because I know you can suffer a lot without showing it," says Grandma.

"Yes, Old Mother. I have been to a *mwalimu* but I am not better."

"What did he do?"

"He wrote Arabic verses in saffron ink inside his bowl, poured water into the bowl to wash out the holy verses and made me drink the mixture."

"The verses could not have been powerful enough –"

"You can do one of two things, Hamisi," Grandfather interrupts.

We all look at Grandfather.

"Go to a *mganga* that Nuri's grandma here went to years ago or –"

"Grandfather of Nuri," Grandma interrupts. "How many times do I have to tell you that there is a difference between a *mganga* and a *mwalimu*. A *mganga* is a quack and I did not go to a quack. I went to a *mwalimu*, a *mwalimu* I say, expert in the Quran, a healer." Then she pretends to mumble to herself, but is just loud enough for us all to hear, "Typical of a *deshi* to mix up *mganga* and *mwalimu*." Grandma calls Grandfather *deshi* because he was born in India and never learned Kiswahili.

"Well, Hamisi, if you wish to go to this, er, expert, you may be cured the way Nuri's Grandmother was cured."

Grandma looks up at Grandfather and wants to say something but does not.

"So this ... this ... er ... expert pressed together the two handles of his pliers and pulled at her stubborn tooth until, *huh, huh*, she fainted."

I look at Hamisi. He does not laugh, so I do not either.

"And the second thing, Old Father?"

"There is a white man. He is a tooth doctor. I don't know anyone who has been to him. They say white men and their children go to him so he must be all right."

"And does he use pliers?" Hamisi asks.

"Aha, he has a magic beyond any magic known to all your *mgangas* and *mwalimus* put together. He gives you a needle and you don't feel a thing."

"What would you do, Old Father?"

"Well, Hamisi, you have tried your Zanzibari medicine and it has not worked. I would not waste any more money on *that* kind of medicine. There is the bicycle. Take it and go. Don't think. The more you think, the more reasons you will find for not doing anything."

Hamisi looks first at Grandfather and then at Grandma and then at Father who must have come into the shop from upstairs to work quietly at his concertina desk in the corner without any of us noticing him. Grandfather nods at Father who motions

Hamisi towards his desk. "My friend Badru," Father tells Hamisi, "says that he has heard Mr. Grant of the Immigration speak highly of this white tooth doctor. So you will be all right." He puts a ten-shilling bill in Hamisi's shirt pocket and says, "Go, Hamisi, go and go now."

I want to wait in the shop until Hamisi returns, but I am aching all over and Grandma says it is time for me to go upstairs for *faki*. Best taken on an empty stomach, she says, first thing in the morning. I follow her to the first floor. Mama Ayah is ready with the horrid mixture. I get it down in two gulps and return the cup to her. She frowns into the cup, says, "Good," smiles at me with a "Not that bad, was it?" and gives me half a cup of chai to wash down the foul taste. Grandma then takes me to the last floor, tucks me in bed and agrees to wake me the moment Hamisi comes back. I begin to drift, not awake, not asleep. I see a long hook-like needle float by. The white doctor holds it above Hamisi who is tied down in bed and gagged with a towel. The many colours of *faki* weave into weird shapes and suddenly explode against the walls of my stomach. I am thrown into my classroom where I try to grab Grandfather's note from Master Rathod's clammy hands because he does not want me to use it again. I rip it off the master's hand and feel the thud of his hand on my forehead. I wake up. Grandma is by my bedside, her hand on my forehead.

"You have been talking in your sleep, Nuri child," she smiles. "Look, what I have brought you."

I sit up and look at the tray in her hands. Coconut soup, my favourite. And fish, *khwana*, better even than *changu* fish. Best of all, floating mountain for pudding. She sits on the bed as I take the tray from her.

"Can I be unwell tomorrow too, Grandma?"

She feels my forehead again, then my cheeks. "For as long as you want to, *beta*."

"And Hamisi, Grandma?"

"He has come and gone."

"But why did no one wake me, Grandma?"

"He was very tired and upset, so I told him to go rest."

"What has he done with his tooth, Grandma?"

"First things first, *beta*," she says, nodding at the tray in my lap.

I blow on the first spoonful of soup, quickly empty it and look at her to start.

"So our Hamisi went to the white *mganga* for white magic, did he?" Grandma begins, hissing as she sucks in her paan juice.

"Well, *beta*, that visit was full of problems," she says solemnly and pauses for me to take the second gulp of soup. "Problem number one was the long wait."

"Were there many people?"

"White customers had to be treated first. That is what the assistant told Hamisi. That is why he took so long coming back."

I take the soup bowl and slurp it empty.

"By the time Hamisi's turn came, the assistant had to go for lunch. That is where we have problem number two. The tooth doctor beckoned Hamisi to take the chair. He was going to treat Hamisi single-handed, without the assistant's help."

Grandma waits until I start on the fish.

"Shall I feed you, *beta*?"

"No, Grandma."

"Where was I, *beta*?"

"Problem number two."

"Yes, problem number two. The tooth doctor has no Kiswahili and Hamisi has no English."

I look up, the morsel of fish half way to my mouth.

"Yes, *beta*, we have come to a high wall. Hamisi on one side and the white *mganga* on the other. Insurmountable."

Grandma's eyes, unblinking, look deep into mine. I think she is pleased that I am enjoying her story. I bring the morsel of rice mixed with curried fish to my mouth. She waits until I begin to chew.

"All our Hamisi could do was to point to where he had the pain. In the lower right jaw, at the back." She opens her toothless mouth and jabs at an invisible tooth. "And that brings us to the biggest problem of all."

She takes her time before beginning again. "We come to the magic that is beyond all known magic, *beta*."

"The needle, Grandma."

"Yes, the needle. Hamisi got the needle, all right." She wipes her mouth and becomes still. Then she shrieks, "But he got it in the wrong place, *ai, ai, ai*. In the upper jaw on the left. Hee, hee hee, hee." And her spongy belly begins to bob.

"What did Hamisi do?"

"Hah, there is only one thing he could do and he did it."

"What, Grandma?"

"The white magician turned his back and Hamisi slipped out of the chair. Holding his heavy jaw in both hands, as if to prevent it from crashing to the floor, he ran for his life. *Wo, wo, wo, wo*."

"But the bicycle?"

"Your father had to go and collect it. And to pacify the tooth doctor."

"And the toothache?"

"His toothache? Oh, he says it no longer hurts. Perhaps he is cured of that toothache. So I was wrong in thinking that his *mwalimu*'s prayers were not powerful enough. They were only slow to take effect."

I start on the floating mountain.

"Only thing is ... he has another toothache instead. In the place where he got the needle."

I look up as I polish off the pudding.

"But there is nothing to worry about, *beta*. I have told him to spend all of your father's ten shillings on his *mwalimu* for a speedier potion."

She looks at me, pleased with herself and with me.

"And now, time for you to get back to sleep."

She takes the tray from me, puts it under the bed and tucks me in.

"Can I go with Hamisi to see the *mwalimu*, Grandma?"

"Whatever for?"

"I am not well and he is better than Dr. Silva."

"You don't need old Silva or a *mwalimu*, child. *Faki* will cure you of what you have."

I suppose I have to get really sick to be able to see the *mwalimu*. Cousin Bablo says the quickest way of raising one's temperature is to put an onion under one's armpit. I forgot to ask him if the onion has to be peeled. He tried the trick once to avoid going to school for a math test. An hour, at least, but longer for high fever signs. He says it is quick, alarms parents and is harmless, apart from the smell. Mama Ayah keeps onions next to potatoes in the big black cupboard outside the kitchen. I feel sleepy, force myself to keep awake, trying to decide if the onion that I must get will need peeling.

I find myself in a dark room with the *mwalimu* sitting cross-legged on the floor in his long *khanzu* dress. His beard reaches the floor and instead of the white cloth cap he has a turban wound up high on his head. He looks at me, the whites of his eyes dripping blood red. He growls for me to sit in front of him. He holds my face in a bruising grip, much more painful than Mother's grip when she combs my hair, and howls Arabic verses into my mouth which he insists I keep open. When my mouth is full of Arabic, he orders me to shut it and swallow all his words in one gulp. As I do so, he grabs a pair of pliers hanging from the ceiling and is about to shove the sharp pointed ends into my mouth.

"You are babbling again, child." I see Mother sitting on my bed. She is smiling. "Have you been dreaming?"

I squeeze the dreaded dream out of my eyes.

"Where is Grandma?"

"She had a busy day today. She is resting downstairs, *beta*."

"I told Grandma I am not well, but I am well, Mother, really well. So can I go to school now?"

"It is still night, *beta*," she laughs. "Tomorrow morning we shall see."

"Truly, Mother, I am well, really I am. I don't want to see the *mwalimu*. I want to go back to school."

"Yes, *beta*, yes." Her hand is on my head.

Emarem

Every time I go out, I have to stop in the shop entrance for Grandfather and Grandma. They look down at my feet. Have I my sandals on? Then they smile up at me to tell them where I am going. Sometimes, when Grandfather is dozing and Grandma is busy talking to a street vendor, I run out in the hope that they will not notice my bare feet. Cheeky rabbit, Grandma cries, and hollers after me loud enough for all the neighbours to hear. I can feel Bhikhoo the tailor in the shop opposite and Kakoo the grocer down the lane having a quiet little laugh as they see me, shamed, shuffling back for my sandals.

"To Uncle Emarem," I say as I stand in the entrance.

"Uncle Emarem is as old as your father, you know that," Grandma reminds me.

"Yes, Grandma."

"So give him proper respect."

"Yes, Grandma."

"And that –"

"– means I do not pester him with too many questions, Grandma," I grin.

She looks at Grandfather, shakes her head and waves me off with a "Go, *beta*, go."

I started going to Uncle Emarem's after the argument Father had
with Mother one night. Mother and I were sitting on the floor in
the front room facing the rocking chair. We were about halfway
through what my brother and sister call "Nuri's audience with
Mother," during which Mother checks my homework, sums first,
and then we go on to talk about the day's happenings. She never
interrupts me. Her eyes brighten and her lips round into an *O*
when I tell her that I found a crab egg on the beach and she
frowns when I tell her about my brother Sham's meanness in
refusing to share the zambarau berries Masi gave him.

On the night of the argument, Father went straight to the
rocking chair. As he passed, he ruffled my hair. I pretended to be
annoyed, though secretly I like it when he does so.

"We should send Nuri to the government school," he began at
once.

Mother looked up, her eyes narrowing into a question.

"A white man, Mr. Evans, teaches English there."

"We should wait until he is a little older," Mother said.

"But he will grow up speaking Indian English," Father said,
his voice rising.

"All I hear is 'Indian English,' as if we are not Indians. We
speak English the way we do and I see no need to be other than
what we are," Mother said. "*You* have done well enough on Indian
English. And when, I ask, will the child learn about our stories
and our ways, hunh?"

"But who could be better than you to teach him our stories
and our ways?" Father said, sounding gentle now.

Mother shook her head. "It's not the same thing. What is more
important, I ask, religion or English?"

"Government school has an additional advantage," Father
persisted. "They teach science there."

"But not Gujarati language or the Khojki script of our
religion."

"That is true," Father yielded. Looking at me, he said, "But
Nuri is a quick learner and can pick up Gujarati and Khojki on his
own."

I felt proud that Father had acknowledged me but was at once also filled with fear that I might be asked to state my preference.

"So why can't he pick up science on his own?"

Father *tched* as if annoyed. "Science requires experiments in a laboratory."

Mother clasped her hands in her lap, sat up straight and pursed her lips into what we all call her thinking *asana*.

"Nuri is only ten," she began softly after a long minute. "We should wait for another year or two, as we did with Sham. And since you feel so strongly about English, why can't we ask your friend Emarem to help?"

Uncle Emarem lives up our lane, near the T-junction. He is short, thin and almost completely bald. I think his bright, light brown eyes are a bit too large for his small head but his little beard, which is bushier and longer than a goat's, gives some sort of a balance to his face. He never gets up before noon and spends the rest of the day either reading at his desk in the entrance of his empty shop area, or talking and arguing until the early hours of the morning with friends and acquaintances whom Grandfather, who does not like Uncle Emarem, regards as victims of chatter. Uncle Emarem's library is in the back room curtained off by a large *khanga* cloth. The room is wider and taller than the school assembly where we meet first thing in the morning for prayers after inspection of our nails and teeth. The library walls are covered with books on the shelves going up to the ceiling and every time I enter I have the feeling of being surrounded by millions of silent words waiting to be smelled, stroked and read. He has more books, which are not in his library. Father says he keeps six huge chests full of his friend's books in our godown. The godown is cool and just right for both Cadbury's chocolates and Uncle Emarem's books.

He does nothing but read when he is on his own.

"No, Nuri, I don't do nothing but read," he said once. "I also think about what I read."

"Can one read without thinking, Uncle Emarem?"

"Oh, yes, child. Ask anyone you know. The important thing, though, is not what you read, but what you think about what you read."

Uncle Emarem is my friend, but nobody knows that, not even Uncle Emarem himself. He never gets annoyed with me. He makes me feel his equal even though he often calls me "child." I feel I can tell him everything and ask him about anything: about the number of stars in the sky, do people live there? About Mama Ayah, why is she black and not brown like us? About his books, do they have all the answers? He never fobs me off, the way I feel Mother and Mama Ayah do when they do not want to be disturbed or when they do not know the answers. As for Father, I do not feel I ought to disturb him with my questions, as he is busy in the shop with his customers and his account books. The long talks I have with him are on serious matters, such as when I want him to buy me a new cricket bat or when Mother suggests I get his consent for learning to ride a bicycle, and then he always questions me on my reasons for wanting what I do and what use I would make of it. And I always feel I have to wait until he is in the right mood, which is usually after a good meal in the afternoon when he is too bloated to think of an excuse to avoid me. Grandma is the only one who is more like Uncle Emarem, though there are some important matters I cannot make her understand, like "googly" or "silly mid on" or "leg before wicket" when I try to explain cricket to her. She thinks the only two ways a batsman has to leave the ground are by being caught or bowled. And sometimes she thinks it best not to know too much, which is the opposite of what Uncle Emarem says when he quotes the Prophet's saying that one should seek knowledge even if one has to go as far as China for it.

I often wonder how Uncle Emarem and Father can be friends. I never see them together for long, but that is perhaps because they cannot meet often, Father being busy in the shop during the day and Uncle Emarem being busy talking at somebody's house at night. They are also different in the way they keep their shops. Father's is full of what Grandma calls junk. High up is a shelf that goes round the three walls with boxes full of forgotten things. Grandma says one box contains old Chinese hand fans which are no longer in fashion, another probably has steel drums, which she thinks were a bad buy, and the three boxes in one corner, she knows, are full of old sewing machine parts that are no longer suitable for new machines.

"So when are you going to get rid of all that junk?" Grandma asks, craning to look at the high shelf and then at Father writing his accounts at his concertina desk.

"Don't call it junk, Ma," Father replies without raising his head, sounding somewhat annoyed.

Grandfather closes his eyes and pretends he is asleep. I know he is pretending because his head is not drooping and his back is as straight as when he is talking or listening.

"Shall I get Hamisi to clear those boxes up?" Grandma asks, looking up at the shelf again.

"No, Ma, no. There is valuable stuff in them."

"Valuable stuff indeed, all preciously preserved in rust and dust."

"I will definitely look into it at the weekend, Ma. Definitely. Yes, definitely."

Grandfather's face is still shut, but his lips have curled up a little.

"Then we will definitely have to wait till the Day of Judgment. Definitely."

Father looks up and stares at Grandma, says nothing and goes back to his account books. Grandfather opens his eyes, rubs his chin and looks out into the lane, lips still curled up. Grandma is the only person who can tell off both Father and Grandfather, and though Grandfather sometimes gets angry with her, Father cannot answer back because she is his mother.

Grandma thinks the junk will not be cleared until my elder brother Sham and I are old enough to take over the business. Faiza, my sister, does not count because when girls get married they belong to another family. Grandma says that when Father took over the shop, he got rid of all the junk that had been piled up by Grandfather before him, except the steel daggers. She thinks Father has now caught the same disease that Grandfather had and hopes and prays that my brother and I do not inherit it.

Uncle Emarem is the opposite of Father. His is really not a shop because there is nothing in it except a leather chair and an old *mbuyu* wood desk with four white steel chairs folded up against one of the walls for visitors. He buys bananas and oranges and eggs and vegetables from street vendors, but he is nowhere near as good as Grandma in choosing what he buys. Nobody can beat Grandma. She feels every mango in the basket, squeezes some too, before choosing the best ones and every egg she picks has to be brought to her right eye to see if the yolk inside is whole and good. I suggest Uncle Emarem get Grandma to buy things for him but he says his needs are very few and simple, though Grandfather thinks he does not need much because he is a scrounger.

In the use of words, though, Father is as good as, perhaps better than, Uncle Emarem. Even Grandma is impressed by what she calls his mesmerizing performance with customers. Father pulls out of the display cupboards jars of Q-ink from England, the *best* ink; multicoloured samples of sandals from Malaya, good *wear* and excellent *value*; booklets of cloth samples from India and Japan, of so many colours that even Father has no names for some of them except "reddish" or "nearer green than yellow"; and the customers have always to *see* the cloth with their *feel*.

Uncle Emarem has got plenty of money, Grandma says, because his father left him a clove plantation ten miles from Stone Town. It is looked after by a manager so that old Emarem does not have to work for money at all.

"Why doesn't Father keep a manager so he does not have to work?" I ask.

"One man not working in this house is more than enough." Grandma looks in Grandfather's direction and laughs. Grandfather has not heard her, or pretends he has not.

I do not know why Grandfather feels so strongly about Uncle Emarem. Grandma thinks that Grandfather, born and brought up in India, is not quite familiar with the lax ways of Zanzibaris. All of us know that he was not happy when Father arranged for me to be taught by Emarem, but he never spoke directly to Father about what his objections were. When he wants to criticize Father, he starts an argument with Grandma within Father's hearing.

"What sort of life is that for a man? How can anyone not want to work?" he asks Grandma while casting sly glances at Father sitting at his corner desk.

"Why should he work? He has enough money to live on."

"And talk, talk, talk, all night long. Contrary to the law of nature, I am saying. Only wild animals are meant to roam about at night and pounce on their prey."

"He makes more sense than I can say for some people," Grandma answers.

"And his shameful criticisms of religion."

"They are not criticisms, Gulu's father. They are genuine doubts about religion. And there is more wisdom in his doubts than in the so-called learning of your farting sheikhs." She laughs a short laugh.

Grandfather stares at her, then clears his throat, pulls the white cotton cap down his head and looks out into the empty lane. After a while he turns to Grandma and murmurs loud enough for Father to hear, "Careful, Nuri's grandmother, we will lose the child."

The first day I went to Uncle Emarem, he gave me a lined exercise book and told me to use it for a permanent record of what I learned.

"Your father tells me that you have a smattering of English. Is that so?" he asked after my salaams, pointing to the chair next to him where I was to sit.

"Yes, Uncle Emarem."

"Give me a few words in English."

"Hands up. Shoot. Gun."

"Can you read or write any English?"

"No, Uncle Emarem."

"Let us start with writing then."

He said letters have sounds and when put together in a particular way they form words. He wrote the letters *N* (*nnn*) and *U* (*oo*) and *R* (*rr*) and *I* (*ee*) in the exercise book, giving each letter its sound and then read the sounds in the order in which he had written the letters, "Nnoorree."

"That is my name, Uncle Emarem."

"Yes, Nuri. Now you write it by tracing on these letters and as you do so, give us the sound of each letter."

"May I write without tracing, Uncle Emarem?"

He stared at me. I thought I had annoyed him, but he smiled and nodded. I wrote the four letters on the line below his writing. My "Nuri" was not as neat as his, but I had written it all on my own.

"Good, Nuri. Now I will write two more letters." He wrote an *M* and an *A*, uttering the sound of each letter as he wrote.

"*Mmm … mmmaaa.* 'Ma,' Uncle Emarem."

"Now write *mmm* and *aaa* and *mmm* and *aaa* and then read the word."

I did what he said. "That is 'Mama,' Mama Ayah's name."

"Good, good, Nuri. How many sounds and letters have we so far?

"One, two … six."

"For your homework, I want you to practise writing these two words and also see if you can form any new words with the letters you have."

"May I do so now, Uncle Emarem?"

He stared at me again but did not seem annoyed.

"Go on."

I wrote *A M I*.

"Well done, Nuri. But 'ami' is a Kiswahili word."

"So I can write Kiswahili also with these letters?"

"Yes, because Kiswahili, unlike Gujarati, is written with the same letters as English."

Suddenly I remembered Father's words to a customer: "What a bargain here. Two for the price of one."

Uncle Emarem is ten Gujarati Master Rathods rolled into one. He shows me pictures in his magazines, picks a word under a picture, gives me the sound of each letter in the word and then tells me its meaning. And he allows me to take home *London Illustrated News* and my favourite, *National Geographic Magazine*. At night Mother and I sit cross-legged on the floor and with her arm round my shoulder, I read her the words under the pictures.

"Igloo. *I* has the sound of *ee*, *G* has the sound of *gh*, *L* has the sound of *luh*, and the two *O*s together have a long *ooo* sound: *eeghloo*," I explain.

Mother moves her finger gently round the dome.

"Doesn't the snow melt?"

"Uncle Emarem says no because it is so cold there." No sense in telling her temperatures in the Eskimo country fall below minus forty Celsius. That is what Uncle Emarem said and I am not sure I have understood it myself.

"They live inside the eeeg ... snow house?"

"Igloo, Mother."

"*Eeghloo*, yes. But none of the pictures show the inside," she says as she removes her arm from my shoulder. Turning the pages, she asks, "How could the snow not melt when they boil their rice inside?"

"No, Mother." I do not know the answer so I make one up. "That is because the snow walls are very thick."

"And another thing. Lavatories, what about their lavatories?"

I never thought of lavatories. She asks good questions.

"I will ask Uncle Emarem."

Some nights I imitate Uncle Emarem, pacing up and down the room, slapping my thigh, and Mother pretends she does not like my making fun of our elders. She says Uncle Emarem has wisdom of the head.

"What is wisdom of the head?"

"He reads a lot and thinks a lot."

"But you don't read a lot, Mother. Have you no wisdom?" She grabs me by the shoulders before I can get away and does not let me free until I admit she has wisdom. Then she explains that there are two types of wisdom, of the head and of the heart, and that wisdom of the heart is not acquired through reading only, but through prayers and good deeds.

One evening in the front room, I tell Mother what Grandfather said to Grandma.

"What does losing me mean, Mother?"

"Your grandfather is very old, and loves you and misses you when you are away and wishes that you would spend more time with him."

"And Father, does he not like Uncle Emarem?"

She gives me the kind of look that I sometimes dread, like when I have done something wrong and her eyes are on me but her mind is working out what I have been up to.

"Whatever makes you say that?" she asks.

"He is always too busy and," I hesitate, then continue, "and when Grandfather complains about Uncle Emarem, Father never defends him."

"Ah," she sighs. "Listen, and listen well. Emarem is your father's best friend. They were at school together and were the brightest students. But, unlike his friend, your father has to work, and sometimes work very hard, because he loves us and because he wants the best education for you and your brother and your sister. Long ago he used to read even more than Emarem but he can do so no more."

She puts her arm round my shoulders and draws me closer. I remember what she said once, that sometimes we talk in silence, without words. She must have meant moments such as this one.

Shortly after starting my lessons with Uncle Emarem, Father announces that he wants my brother Sham to help me in my lessons. I know nothing will come of it because I do not get on well with him. He often reminds me that I am five years, one month and a day his junior. I admit he once came to my rescue when I was being threatened by the school bully Ghoondo, but, apart from that, he never bothers about me unless he wants me to do something for him, like running an errand or keeping his secret, like when I caught him smoking Grandfather's asthma cigarettes on the third floor. Another of Father's ideas is that I will learn English more quickly if my sister Faiza will read to me at least one English story a week and explain difficult words. She thinks all the words are difficult for me, but I think she herself does not know the meanings of many words and is too lazy to look them up in her *New Method English Dictionary*. She never stops for me to look at the pictures in a book and never answers my questions. When I am by myself, I make up my own stories from the pictures and then tell them to Mother. Mother does not believe grass can be as green as in the pictures because even after the long *masika* rains the grass is never so green. And she thinks the ice-cream snow on mountain tops is all a fairy tale because the ice blocks we buy from Sodawalla look nothing like the soft white of the snow in the book. But she says she likes the stories I make up. The pictures are all of people who are either brown like us or white like Europeans and I can point to some old man on a mountain as the Prophet Moses climbing up to talk to God, or the eyebrows forming arches on the face of a girl like those of the beautiful Queen Sita waiting for her Lord Rama. None of the pictures is of black boys and girls and I cannot therefore make up stories like Mama Ayah's about Mwana Kupona the way Mama Ayah does. In any case, the stories I make up are better than the real ones Faiza reads.

I am glad Uncle Emarem is my teacher. With the sounds of the letters he teaches, I can also read some Kiswahili words. English is more difficult though and I have to remember when two different letters have the same sound, as with *C* in "come" and *K* in "*karibu.*"

"'*Karibu*' means 'welcome,'" Uncle Emarem says and writes the English word for me. "Now say it after me, 'welcome.'"

"Velcome," I repeat.

"No, Nuri. *W* does not have the sound of *V* but the sound of *W*." He rounds his lips and waits for me to imitate him.

He teaches me to write three new words every session and to read one or two more words under the pictures in his magazines.

Father has started taking greater interest in what I am learning and sometimes joins my evening talks with Mother. I think he wants me to be able to pronounce English words the way the English do, though I am not sure he can tell if I am succeeding.

When I tell Father about Uncle Emarem's books, he says that I can build a library as big as I want once I am grown up. I ask him what Emarem means.

"The three letters," he says as he takes my exercise book and writes *M R M.*"

"*Em, aar, em.* Emarem, Father."

"*M* for 'most.' *R* for 'read.' And *M* again for 'man.'"

"Most read man," I repeat.

"Yes, Nuri, he is the most well-read man in Zanzibar."

I continue looking at the letters.

"You seem disappointed, Nuri." Father puts his hand under my chin and lifts my head.

"Only in Zanzibar?"

"Maybe you are right. I have not yet met anyone in the whole world who is as well read as your Uncle Emarem."

"Can I see Allah, Uncle Emarem?"

His eyes come together and his thick eyebrows seem bushier. He strokes his beard slowly, which means he is thinking. He lifts his long white *khanzu* shirt, takes out a small handkerchief from his white pajama pants, wipes his bald head, then looks into the distance. I begin to wonder if the question is too difficult. But I know he likes difficult questions. Maybe it is the heat.

"Tell me, Nuri, you must have given the matter some thought?"

"Yes, but –"

"Tell us," he interrupts.

"When I was little, I thought Allah must be like Grandma. I could say anything to Him and ask anything. Only He never told anyone off for asking questions."

He slaps his thigh, rolls up his eyes, rubs his bald head hard and from deep inside him comes a loud, frightening "hah."

"And now?" he asks, glaring into my eyes.

I want to, but do not, tell him that Allah has to be like him.

"You do say your daily prayers, don't you?" he asks, his eyes still fixed on me.

I nod.

"And every time you *know* He is there?"

I nod again.

"You *feel* He is there listening to your prayers."

"Sometimes."

"If you *know* He is there, and if you *feel* Him, sometimes at any rate ..." He pauses, leans forward, his face now close to mine, lips pressed thin, eyes ready to burst. He slams hand against his thigh and thunders, "Does it *matter* if you do not see Him the way you see *me*?"

Sometimes I am not sure I understand.

"Feeling, knowing. Is that not a kind of seeing?" He looks at me as if expecting a reply.

"Like my talking to Mother without speaking?"

He bursts out laughing. "Yes, yes, Nuri."

"When I can read your books, will I know the answers?"

"More than that, Nuri, more than that. You will be able to question the answers."

"Question the answers?"

"Yes, Nuri, yes."

"When will I be able to read your books?"

"Not too long, Nuri, not too long."

I am looking at the photograph of the Empire State Building in a picture book and wondering how any building could be so much taller than our own four-storeyed House of Wonders with its tall tower, when I feel Uncle Emarem's eyes on me. I look up.

"It all began with one word, Nuri."

I like to hear him talk about difficult things. I close the picture book gently, the way he always does.

"Do you know how Allah created the world?"

I shake my head.

"He said '*kun*,' which means 'be,' and there was the world."

He is watching me.

"Out of nothing?"

"In a sense, yes, Nuri. '*La*' means 'no' and we can make it to mean 'nothing.' Out of nothing, yes. Now take 'word.'" He spells it. "Include in it the letter *L* for '*la*.' What do you get?"

He watches as I work on the puzzle. Wordl. Lword.

"'World'?"

"Yes, Nuri, yes. The word into the world."

"But –"

"But what Nuri?"

"But 'la' is Arabic and 'word' is English."

"Why should God not mix up languages if He wants to?" He starts pacing, arms behind him.

"Is God like us then, the way we mix up Kiswahili and Kutchi?"

He stops pacing, rubs his cheek and says, "Now that is an idea. Perhaps He is."

He chuckles and starts pacing again. He is in a good mood and I decide to ask questions that one would not normally ask of one's elders.

"Why are some people bald, Uncle Emarem?"

He stops again. "You mean why *Emarem* is bald?"

I giggle.

"There could be many causes, Nuri, and I don't know for sure. In my case it is probably due to age."

"But why you and not Grandfather?"

"That, Nuri, is Allah's will."

"How do you know?"

"What do you think?"

"From your books?"

"No, Nuri," he laughs. "Sometimes I do not know the answer so I invent the one I like. I can always change it if I find a better answer."

He sits in his chair.

I tell him what Father thinks *MRM* stands for.

"And what do you think?"

"Yes."

"Yes, what?"

"Yes, you are the most well-read man in the world," I say.

"Huh, so it is the world now, is it? Tell me, why do you think so?"

"The books in your library. There are more here than there are books in the Kiponda library."

"Not more, Nuri. More selective, certainly." He strokes his beard as he looks out into the lane, then turns to me again solemnly.

"If you pile up books on a donkey, would you say the donkey is well read?"

"But you have read them all?"

"I suppose I should let you in on a secret." He bends forward and starts speaking as if he does not want anyone close by to hear even though we are the only persons in the shop.

"All the books in my library ..." He looks at his hands, then his nails. "Truth to tell, I have not read them all."

"But, but you know everything in those books."

"Yes, Nuri, that is true. I think I do know what is in all of them though I have not read them all."

I am puzzled.

"I lend books, Nuri, the way I lend picture and storybooks to you. And what do you do?"

"I read them."

"Yes, but when you return the books, what is our arrangement?"

"You ask me questions and I explain."

"Exactly. I do the same with some of my books. One lifetime is not enough to read everything one wants to. So I buy and lend books to anyone intelligent and curious enough to want to read them. But always on one condition. He must read the book and tell me what the author says and answer my questions. If he does not, or cannot, he does not get my books."

He stares into my eyes and begins again, "Allah has blessed me with a good memory. Not perhaps as good as yours, mind you, but better than average, much better. I remember much of what I read or hear."

"Do the others know, Uncle Emarem?"

"Your father does."

I begin to think even more highly of Father who has never told the secret to anyone, not me, not Mother, not Grandma and certainly not Grandfather.

"Some think I am more learned than I am and others think I am full of hot air. What is important is that one should always be oneself."

"Can one be other than oneself?"

"Yes, Nuri, as when one pretends to be what one is not in order to impress others. Or when a man behaves in a way others expect him to rather than the way he himself would like to."

I look at Uncle Emarem but he is now away in his thoughts. I wait for his return.

"Hurry up with your English and Gujarati, Nuri," he says at last, standing up. He walks from his desk to the wall and back again, nodding every now and then. Without looking at me, he says, "Then between the two of us we can read twice as much as either of us can do on his own. Imagine, Nuri, imagine understanding, not merely reading, but understanding, how the word became the world."

I like Uncle Emarem when he is full of bubbles, even when I do not understand what he means. But I know that one day I will understand him when he tells me what he has read and I will tell him what I have read and he will understand me in turn. And I will read a lot, lots more than Uncle Emarem, and I will not let others read for me. I will read even more than Father did long ago and make up for Father so that he will be proud that I am able to do what he always wanted to do himself. And if I have doubts, which Uncle Emarem always says is the starting point of learning, even doubts about religion, then I will make sure that my doubts will have as much wisdom as Uncle Emarem's. One day I will understand how the word became the world. One day soon. Uncle Emarem has promised.

BBC English

Every now and then the moods descend on Grandma but they do not stay with her long and leave her as suddenly as they come. They make her angry, she says, but instead of shooing away the moods, she bawls at those around her. One sure sign of the onset of these moods is when she speeds up chewing the paan in her toothless mouth, and from the low stool in the shop entrance her cat eyes search for prey to pounce on. Everyone tries to keep out of her way, though they all know she means no harm. She has never let her moods loose on me, but that is because she thinks I am still a child. Even the street vendors can feel her moods and try to quicken their dawdling as they approach our shop, but that only doubles the speed at which she chews her paan.

"So I am not good enough for your mangoes, is it?" she hollers at Salimu who comes to a sudden stop, raising his arms in a panic to steady the basket balanced on his head. He gives her his white smile and says in a shy voice, "But they are not quite ripe, Mama."

"Not quite ripe indeed. Who is going to eat them, you or me? Come here and let me see them."

Salimu shuffles towards her, lowers his basket on the stone step and allows her to choose her fruit. On the day of the moods, he never argues with her for being too picky, or for digging deep into his basket, or for grumbling that his mangoes are too soft or too green or too rotten for humans.

Poor Grandfather is always her first victim, because he is old and cannot help dozing off on the wooden bench facing her. When Brahmin Bapa passes by in his spotless white shirt and *dhoti*, vegetable cloth bag in hand, and greets Grandfather with his "*dua*," Grandfather jerks up, returns the greeting, cranes forward, narrows his eyes on the Brahmin and asks Grandma in a whisper, "Who was that?"

"*Ho, oh, heh, heh*," Grandma cries. "Who is this and who is that. Why don't you wear your glasses?"

Everyone knows Grandfather's glasses are for reading *Zanzibar Voice*, the daily Gujarati news-sheet, and not for dozing. He raises his shoulders, pushes himself back into his bench and turns to look out into the lane as though she were not there.

"Questions, questions. All day long. As if I have nothing better to do."

"The devil's workshop, I say," Grandma begins one day. The slow bites into her paan mean that she is not yet possessed by the moods but is only complaining about the brown box radio that Father bought a week or so ago. "And turned on daily before evening prayers too," she grumbles, as if she herself says her evening prayers on time every day. Her jaws begin to work faster on the paan but I am not sure if the moods have begun to possess her. She is certainly not talking to herself, as she sometimes does when she is on her own, because even though her face is turned towards the beads cupboard to the right, the blacks of her eyes have almost disappeared in the left of her eyes as she looks at Father at his concertina desk in the corner. Father does not reply and continues to look at his papers.

The only person who listens to the radio before prayer time is Leli Aunty who has come to Zanzibar from the mainland to give birth to her first baby. That is the custom, she says, for the first child to be born at one's mother's house. She is even fatter than she was before she got married but that is because, she says, she is pregnant. I wonder what she does with all the clothes she cannot get into. She is the last of Grandma's children and when she lived with us until her marriage last year, she saved all the frocks she got too fat for. The black antique corner cupboard on the first floor is still full of her old clothes. Grandma says that when you want something, really want something, and die without having it, you have to be reborn to get it. Something to do with unfulfilled desires standing in the way of the soul's journey to its destination. But, Grandma adds, that reason for being reborn is quite separate from having to return to pay for all the hurt one causes others in this life. I am certain Leli Aunty will never again be thin enough in this life to get into the frocks she has coveted. Not because she is pregnant, but because she has given up on her fasting bouts that so annoyed Grandma before she got her daughter engaged and then married off to Hasnu Uncle. Aunty was twenty-three by then, which is very old, because Mother got married at fifteen and Grandma at fourteen. I am afraid Leli Aunty will have to be reborn, certainly to fit herself into her frocks again, but also very likely to pay for her bursts of nasty temper in this life. I wonder what she will look like in her next life. I cannot see her as thin, and certainly not permanently honeyed, though she can be quite pleasant when she wants to.

"The box should never have been bought. No need for it," Grandma continues her grumble. This time she bends forward and looks directly towards the concertina desk so that Father can see her. He pushes his glasses up the bridge of his nose with his index finger and begins to write but I think he is only pretending that he has not heard her.

The radio has taken the place of the old phonograph on the table by the window on the first floor. At Mother's insistence, the phonograph was sent off to Father's godown to avoid cluttering up the front room. The box has a knob that can be tuned to stations as far away as New Delhi, Berlin and London. Father tried playing with it for the first few days but has not bothered with it again for the whole of this week. I gave up on it the first day, as I could not understand the language on any of the stations. The only time it is switched on now is for the *Your Favourites* program broadcast on All India Radio. Leli Aunty removes the white crochet cover from the box, fiddles with the knob until the music comes on, but then leaves the room to get ready for mosque. All our neighbours can hear the music because the lane we live in is narrow, so narrow that we can talk to those who live opposite us. That is why I think nobody I know has a telephone. The nearest phone is at the police station by Darajani Bridge where I sometimes see the barefooted policeman in his tarboosh turning the handle on the box and then booming into the speaker.

One day, when All India Radio played "*Meri jaan, meri jaan*," Bikhoo the tailor in his shop opposite stopped whirring his sewing machine, looked up and hollered the way he used to when the old phonograph needed winding up, "Nuri, ai Nuri, turn up the volume, *yaar*." Leli Aunty heard him. Rushing back into the room, she turned off the radio, went to the window and shouted back at Bikhoo, "*Our* radio and you order *us*? *Sala*, what do you think we are? Your servants? And bullying a little boy. Have you inherited a donkey's brains?" I went to the middle window just in time to see Bhikhoo cower over his sewing machine and start pedalling as if possessed by an evil spirit. The fun did not last long, because Aunty then turned on me with a voice loud enough for Bikhoo and all the neighbours to hear: "And where are your brains, henh? Getting others to order you about?" Her eyes became frighteningly red before she waddled her fat out of the room.

Nobody argues with Aunty, apart from Grandma. It's just as well that her husband, Hasnu Uncle, can get out of her way and have a long break at the bank where he works as an accountant. But she does look pretty in the evenings, in a soft sort of way, in her loose ankle-length *khanga* dress, all puffed up in the cane rocking chair. She smiles for me when I bring her thick brewed masala chai from the kitchen and does not tell me off for spilling it into the saucer. I wait to see her slurp up several saucerfuls, hoping that she might allow me to feel or hear the child inside her as she sometimes does. No point asking her to allow me to do so, because she never agrees to let me do what I want if I ask her. The best move is to stand quietly by and smile at her when she looks at you, and once in a while, though not all the time, look at her tummy.

Mother has washed zambarau berries in saltwater and placed them in a wooden bowl on the dining table. The darker the zambarau purple, the sweeter it tastes. I choose the best ones and put them on my side. Father comes and sits opposite me and takes two of the fattest and firmest of my berries and plops one into his mouth. He always waits until I have chosen enough of the best of whatever is going, berries or lychees or whole cashews, and then either pounces on my best picks or asks me to give him some. I once complained to Mother about his meanness but Mother told me to eat my best ones first so that Father could get only the leftovers. I should have known she would take his side. She always does.

"I want you to be good in English," Father says as he removes the zambarau stone from his mouth and drops it into the brass bowl that is on the table for that purpose. He pops the second berry into his mouth and stretches to pick another of my selections. I stare at him.

"Yes," he says, completely ignoring my stare. "English is important."

"But Master Rathod says I am good in English." I finally decide to stop picking berries from the bowl and start eating from my own pile before Father finishes the lot.

"But I want you not only to read English well, but also to speak it well."

"Why can't we wait for Uncle Emarem to return from India? He was the best, Father."

"I know. He was a good teacher to you. But we don't know when the doctors will let him return."

He picks the last of my berries and turns it round between his thumb and index finger, the way Grandma does while poor Salimu the street vendor waits for her to make up her mind about his produce.

"You should hear Master Rathod speak, Father. Pukka Indian English."

He pops the berry into his mouth.

"I do not want you to talk disrespectfully of your teacher, Nuri. Now listen. I want you to understand what the English say, and you can do that only by listening carefully to the way they speak."

He starts rolling the berry in his mouth.

"That is why I have bought the radio," he continues as he bites into the berry. I stare at the space on my side of the table, now empty.

"So that you can listen in to the BBC, Nuri."

"But –"

"Yes, you must listen to the BBC news every day and then tell me all about it."

"But –"

He interrupts again and narrows his eyes on me. He always does that to stop me from looking away, as if by looking away I might think of a good reason for not doing what he wants me to.

"Wouldn't it be better, Father, if I saw more of the English-speaking movies instead?"

"Once in a while, yes. But BBC is English."

Before I can tell him that Jesse James and Wyatt Earp also speak English, he gets up, spits the zambarau stone straight into the brass bowl and says, "Time for my afternoon rest. BBC news broadcast is on at three every afternoon. You can start from, let us say, tomorrow. And then report to me what you hear."

"Father wants me to listen to the BBC news," I tell Bablo who is down on all fours looking for the right jigsaw bits for the thousand-piece Big Ben puzzle spread out on the floor. He sits up on his knees and looks at me. I do not look at him but I can feel his eyes opening wide and both hands covering his mouth.

He does that whenever he is taken by surprise either by anything I say or by something I show him, like the lizard I once pulled out of my pocket during school recess.

"Father thinks it is a good idea for you to join me," I lie as I stare at the gaps in Big Ben. I know Bablo cannot refuse because his grandfather and mine are cousins who came to Zanzibar from India and Father is therefore his uncle.

"But why me?"

"He says it will improve our English."

He picks up a jigsaw piece and stares at it. "But isn't old Rathod enough for us?"

"Father says Master Rathod's English is not *English* English."

"Then let Master Rathod listen to the BBC." He takes a deep breath, which means he is worried. "We haven't got much English to improve on, Nuri," he whimpers.

"I said that to Father," I lie again, "but he says it will do us no harm. He says he bought the radio specially for our education."

"What does Grandma say?"

"I don't think she knows. Maybe Father thinks the exercise he has set for us might get her to abandon her war against the box."

Bablo puts down the piece in his hand and picks up another one, bending over to fit it into Big Ben. Still with his hands on his knees, he says, "We are only beginners, Nuri. How can we understand BBC English?"

"We see English-speaking pictures at the Empire Cinema."

"But that is different. The story is told in pictures and even if we don't understand the words, we make up our own stories from them, though yours are sheer fantasy."

"Yes, yes, we all know what an English expert *you* are. An authority on the subject. Not to speak of the *lapsi*-mush you make of the Hindi films."

"Ho, ho, so now we have a Hindi expert who cannot say two Hindi words without slipping a Kiswahili one in between."

"We have a problem, Bablo." I do not want to quarrel with him.

"You got that right, Nuri."

We sit cross-legged on the floor, staring in silence at the Big Ben puzzle, which like our English is still full of gaps.

"When does he want us to start?" Bablo asks, without looking up.

"Today, at three."

"That is now?"

"Yes."

"You idiot, Nuri. What are we sitting here for?"

"Suppose we get the news all wrong? Or not get it at all?" Bablo asks as I set the radio needle to London.

"Father says he will understand. He thinks we should get it after some time. After we get used to the way *English* English sounds, that is."

"How long is 'after some time,' Nuri?"

"I don't know."

"Do you think Uncle understands BBC English?" he asks.

"Of course he does. Doesn't he type all those letters? And the number of English books he has in his shelf."

"Yes, but we are talking about the way the English speak, Nuri, not writing or reading."

I have never heard Father talk to a white man. The only time he came anywhere near to speaking to one was when the white nun from the convent school came to the shop wanting to buy rosary beads. Father and Grandma started talking in gestures, Grandma far less shy than Father, until the nun started speaking in Kiswahili. Best that Bablo does not know.

I check the radio to see if I have set the needle on the right station. Just as the BBC starts, so does the argument in the next room between Leli Aunty and Grandma. Grandma is insisting that Leli Aunty should have *goondhpaak*, good especially for pregnant women, made from the best jaggery and gum Arabic and almonds and lashings of ghee. Leli Aunty says nothing of the sort is in her pregnancy books, and Grandma cries her own experience is worth ten times Aunty's books, and Aunty cries back that Grandma is old-fashioned, and Grandma replies that the authors of the books cannot speak with the same authority as someone like Grandma with the number of children she has given birth to.

Our first reports to Father are that neither Bablo nor I have understood anything of the BBC news. We do not mention Grandma-Aunty's side broadcast.

"It has taken them a thousand years to speak the way they do now," Father says.

"That means we have to be patient," I tell Bablo when we are on our own.

"Just as well Uncle is understanding," Bablo says. "I only hope we don't have to listen in for another thousand years before we can speak BBC."

"We will never make it, Nuri, " says Bablo, during our second week.

"Maybe you concentrate too hard, Bablo."

"How else can I catch what is being spoken?"

The problem, Bablo thinks, is not our poor vocabulary but the speed at which the BBC man reads English, while I think the problem is the accent which is flat and spoken as if the reader has a permanent cold.

"I have been thinking about it, Bablo."

"What?"

"Why not first listen to the news in Hindi on All India Radio?"

"What? With our Hindi?"

"Why not, Bablo? We are bound to understand at least some of it."

"That's brilliant, Nuri. We don't have to bother with the BBC then."

"No, you fool. We also listen in to BBC as Father says and see if we catch anything on BBC that matches All India Radio."

"Brilliant," Bablo repeats. "But won't he catch us when he checks his Gujarati news-sheet?"

"Only if we are completely out, Bablo. In any case, he is not likely ever to find out." I tell him that Father hardly reads the Gujarati news-sheet which is delivered at the shop early in the afternoons when he is having his little rest. Bhikhoo the tailor borrows it from Grandfather and reads it whilst picking his teeth, then passes it next door to Samji the *khanga* merchant who in turn hands it over to Kakoo the grocer. By the time the news-sheet is brought back to the shop late in the evening by Chongo, the one-eyed watch repairman, Father is already out.

"He is talking about Korea," I say as we sit close to the radio.
    "Where is Korea?"
    "Shut up, Bablo."
    "Something about a war?"
    "Yes."
    "What else?"
    "I don't get it."
    "But your Hindi is supposed to be better than mine, Nuri."
    "Shush, Bablo, listen."
    "To the war in the next room or the one in Korea?"
Grandma and Leli Aunty have their regular arguments at the same time as our broadcasts. Today they are arguing about where Aunty should deliver her baby. The hospital, she insists, and Grandma cries never, that she has already made arrangements with Old Dhai who helped deliver all her children at home and that no doctor, and she does not care where trained, could have the same experienced hands as Old Dhai.

"We must now wait and see if BBC has anything on Korea," I say.

"The war in Korea is getting bloody," I report to Father.
    "Deaths?" he asks.
    "He didn't say."
    "You mean you didn't get it."
I look down at the floor.
    "Anything else in the news?"

"Yes, but we still don't understand much, Father."

"Not to worry. As long as you give me one news item every time."

When nothing on the BBC matches any of the news on All India Radio, Bablo and I make up a news item of our own by repeating in a different way the previous day's news. Father seems not to notice or to mind. We certainly made up the news on the day Old Dhai came to deliver Leli Aunty's baby boy in the room next door. Locked by Grandma in the radio room, we could not see anything of the delivery through the crack in the closed door and wondered how a newborn babe could cry louder than either of us and, when at last allowed to look at the baby, at how Grandma and Aunty and Mother could possibly think that the toothless thing was so beautiful.

The neighbours have become interested in the news broadcasts of All India Radio. Bhikoo the tailor asks me to keep the volume loud enough for him to hear, but "without a word to the dragon." Samji and Kakoo also meet at Bhikoo's at news time and then compare what is said on "Nuri's radio" with what the news-sheet has. I feel proud when they say that "Nuri's radio" is more up to date.

"We are really thick, Nuri." Bablo's eyes shine up when he thinks he is having one of his brilliant ideas.

"What now?"

"Why don't we check the news-sheet first? We can read Gujarati."

"Genius, Bablo."

We try to get the news-sheet but do not succeed, as whoever has it shoos us off because he has not finished reading it.

"Back to All India Radio then," Bablo says.

"You and your brilliant ideas."

We hear a short Hindi news item on the Festival of Britain. There is peace in the middle room next door where Aunty, flat out on Grandma's bed, has a string tied to her toe for rocking the baby's cradle every time she jerks up from her doze. A longer news item follows on the BBC.

"There's a Festival of England," Bablo begins his report to Father. I am about to correct him with "Festival of Britain," but do not, as Father does not object.

"The king and the queen went to the church where the bells were ringing," I say.

"And then they joined the crowds in London's streets," Bablo takes up from me. "And they started dancing with the crowds," Bablo continues. I push my elbow hard into his side. The fool is unstoppable. "Dancing and beating the drums. *Dhoom, dhoom, dhoom.* In their turbans, beating their drums and dancing with open swords in their hands like."

Abrupt stop. Too late. Father calls both of us to his side. Tweaks our ears hard and long. I see Bablo go pink. Neither of us cries.

Grandma's moods have not descended on her for a long time. Bablo thinks he knows the reason. The radio, he says, has been sent off to the godown and the old phonograph has been brought back. I think the true reason her moods are gone is Grandma's relief at Leli Aunty's departure. Arguing tires her, particularly with someone like Leli Aunty who thinks she is modern and therefore always in the right, or even with someone like Grandfather who, she constantly complains, is selectively deaf. With Leli Aunty's departure, Bhikhoo the tailor has gone back to hollering, "Wind it up, Nuri *yaar*," whenever the phonograph slows down to a flagging drone. But there is a faraway cloud. Father has threatened to bring back the box in a year's time when I start attending government school.

Revolutionary

I meander to a stop some distance from our shop, then move to the opposite side of the narrow lane and crane my head. No trace of the upside-down chair in the entrance, the shopkeeper's sign that he is asleep or away or just unavailable. I shuffle forward. I must have timed it all wrong. The idea is to get back home when everyone is flattened insensible with lunch and heat, then to sneak into the house without anyone noticing my bare feet. I just do not understand Grandma's insistence that I put on footwear, "shoes are best," whenever I go out. I tell her none of my friends do. Her standard response to anything she does not want to agree with is: "And if all of them jumped into a dry well, will you do so too?"

There is Hamisi, leaking sweat. So he is guarding the open entrance, resting on the floor against the right half-door, head back, mouth open, exhaling a long *soooo* for every gentle *nkhrrr* he inhales. He always sits against the male half of the door, facing Grandma's low stool set down by the female half. That is something else I do not understand: why the right half-door should be male and the left one female. That males are right- and females left-handed cannot be true because Uncle Emarem is left-handed. I once asked Grandma to explain the puzzle. We eat, Grandma said, and give and take gifts and do most of the work with the right hand, and so silly people have come to believe that the right male door is a sign of all that is strong and the left female door of all that is weak. She called such belief a prejudice, and when I asked why there should be such prejudice against women she said that prejudices are always without reason, which is exactly why they are prejudices.

I dig into my pockets, take out the charm, a narrow black cloth band with a small piece of *vigani* tied in a knot in the middle. Held close to one's nose, *vigani* reek produces a shudder. Grandma insists I wear it always, on my right arm, above the elbow because a *mwalimu* has sprayed prayers on it for protection against evil spirits. But I slide it off when I go out, as do my friends. Bablo is the only exception. He wears his charm all the time, but instead of *vigani* his charm has a piece of writing folded enough times into a little diamond and then knotted up in a black cloth band. He says that a mouthful of prayers breathed onto the paper gives it a special potency. Better my *vigani*, though, than his paper charm. Arabic prayers in saffron ink get blurred when the paper gets wet, through rain or seawater or just perspiration, and then they lose their power. *Vigani* is better by far. Its *pong* has a more pungent *phooh* once it's wet, gaining in power, until the reek gets too strong even for the elders, and then the time is right for a new one.

I get the charm ready to swing across Hamisi's face, for protection against being informed on, but then decide not to because Hamisi is in his afternoon stupor. In any case he would not tell on me. In all the years I have known Hamisi, which is forever, he has never betrayed me, not even when he has caught me sneaking out of the house barefooted.

Grandma knows all about Hamisi. Her truth is best, unlike Grandfather's, which consists only of facts. Grandma's is unzipped, unframed like the fading picture of the winged horse Buraq on the wall above her hard afternoon mattress on the second floor, ready for the Prophet's ascent to Heaven. Hamisi came, she says, before I was born. The day was Friday. She had completed her early morning prayers, with the sun about to come and start shadows to replace the cool of the departing night. An old man, older than Grandfather, in flowing *khanzu*, white, appeared at the main entrance, walking stick in left hand, a child hanging on to his right. Could it really be Rajabu, her childhood friend, the grandson of a freed slave? She had not seen Rajabu since she was carried off from the beach when her parents agreed to her engagement to Grandfather, never to play with her friends again. The child was Hamisi, and Rajabu had come to leave his son with Grandma to be looked after, to be trained as a servant. She had just risen from the last prostration in her prayers. The day was Sabbath. How could she refuse?

I look at my bare feet, then at Hamisi's face, sweat drops merging, worming down to his chin dimple. I only wish he did not waste his afternoons dozing. I slide the charm up my arm, move towards the staircase, then stop. What was it that Grandma said last night? She was still in my bed, where she always begins the night, releasing herself from my clamping arms when she thinks I am asleep, tip-toeing to her own bed, sometimes to Grandfather's.

"It's Hamisi," her paan-muffled voice.

"He is not well?" Grandfather's voice.

"No, it's not that."

"He wants more money?"

"It's never about money with Hamisi. You know that."

"Then what?"

"I am not sure. He seems, er, subdued."

"Lazy you mean. All *karias* are lazy."

Whenever Grandfather comes up with his "All blackies are lazy," Grandma bawls back with her "When will you stop shitting on the land that feeds you?" or "When will you stop taking credit for being born an Indian?" But this time I felt Grandma stop breathing, her belly unyielding leather.

"Gulu's mother," Grandfather's voice, after a pause, now gentle. "He is a good man. Fret not. It will pass."

She had started breathing again.

I am not sure if Grandfather means what he says about Hamisi because I have often seen him ask Hamisi to take breaks from his chores. In any case, I must try once more to get Hamisi to agree to learn to read and write and prove to everybody that he spends his afternoons studying instead of sleeping as all the other grown-ups do. I turn round and walk back to him. I only wish he could believe what I have told him several times, that all he has to do is remember the sounds of the alphabet.

I lower my head to his right ear, then whisper, "I say, Hamisi."

He does not stir. I stand back. Hands cupped round mouth, I whisper again, louder, "I say, Hamisi."

His left eye opens wide, his face unmoving. The huge black of the eye rotates slowly towards me. The lid shuts.

"Wake up, Hamisi."

A twitch on his right cheek breaks the even flow of perspiration on his face. Both eyes open. Both are about to close when I leap across his outstretched legs. Shaking him by his shoulders, I mutter through clenched teeth, "You can't sleep, Hamisi. You can't waste your time."

"Leave me alone, little monster," he moans.

"Don't call me little, Hamisi," I say, letting go of his shoulders. "I go to the secondary school, I will have you know."

"I've had a hard day, Nuri," he croaks.

"It will be harder if you don't learn to read and write in your spare time."

"Tomorrow, Nuri."

"Always tomorrow with you. This is my last offer. Either you start now or never."

"Not now, Nuri. Later."

"When later, Hamisi?"

"When the day's work is done."

"Swear it."

"Go away, Nuri."

"Swear it, Hamisi."

His right hand swishes limply under his chin as he says, "*Wallahi*, Nuri."

"Aha, Hamisi," I cry, shaking my forefinger at him. "This is very serious. You have taken Allah's name. Yes, very serious. Today then. When the day's work is done."

He folds up his legs, arms round knees, then shakes his head. "It won't do, Nuri, I was in my sleep."

"You can't shake your head out of this one, Hamisi."

Halfway towards the staircase, I look back. "Before you go out for your evening prayers, Hamisi."

Hamisi hesitates, then whimpers, "*Inshallah.*"

That should please Grandma. And prove to everyone, as if proof were needed, that Hamisi is neither lazy nor dense. The truth is that Hamisi works the hardest of us all, certainly harder than Father. The only thing Father ever does is sit in his swivel chair in the shop, write accounts, type letters and spend time talking to customers. Nothing to compare with Hamisi's chores: wash and iron clothes, run errands for everyone, go to the godown to receive and arrange crates ordered by Father from England, Japan and India, go to the post office four or more times to clear the mailbox when a large foreign ship is in the harbour, always at the beck and call of everybody, including guests, even when some of them call him, in Grandma's absence, "Boy." He starts the day with Grandma before anyone else in the house is up. Father is the last one to get out of bed and that is not because of the arrival of the heavy-footed Pitu the barber, but because of Grandma's hollering, "Gulu, ai Gulu, Pitu is here d'you hear, Guloo, Gooloo …," which does not stop until he stumbles down the stairs and drops into his chair in the shop where Pitu waits to shave him. Sometimes Pitu bleeds him with cuts from the long razor. "To make sure he stays awake," Grandma laughs.

I go up the flight of wooden stairs that open into the second-floor middle room. Grandma, eyes closed, mouth bulging with paan, is asleep on her hard mattress on the springless bed. I have never seen her without paan in her mouth. Even when gobbling down her morsels of rice and gallons of thick brewed chai, the paan always returns undisturbed from somewhere inside her cheek. I wait for her to bite into the paan in her sleep and then, noiseless, climb up the steep wooden stairs to the last floor. I am the only one who spends quiet afternoons up here. Everyone else, including Hamisi, finds it unbearably hot under the corrugated iron roof. *Moto Jahanum*, hell hot, they say.

The stairs end on the third floor with the verandah to the right open to the cloudless sky. As always, I wait by the verandah door, a habit almost, hoping, expecting, to see *Ghar Dhani*, Master of the House, the way sister Faiza claims she once did. He was sitting cross-legged, she says, amidst the rose and jasmine bushes planted by Grandma in earthen pots lining the four walls. A large black Hindu with long grey hair reaching his waist. "How do you know he is a Hindu?" "He was wearing his *dhoti*, silly." He must have owned the house before we moved in and though he is dead, he does not wish to leave. It is *Ghar Dhani* who is responsible for doors in the house remaining open all day and all night. Mother and Father heard knocks on their bedroom door several nights running, she says, stabbing the air with her knuckles on invisible doors. No one was there, no one they could see. That was *Ghar Dhani's* way of saying he wanted the doors kept open. None of the doors has since been shut, except for the bathroom ones. "And the two half-doors of the shop entrance at night," I add, pleased with her irritation at my having got in the last word.

The afternoon is steamy, still. *Ghar Dhani* is not on the verandah. Why is he called *Dhani*, Master, anyway? I go into the vast bedroom with its five beds along three walls. My own bed is by the window in the centre. During *masika*, I can hear the unrelenting rain pound down the corrugated iron roofs, become a roaring waterfall and then form a shallow rivulet covering the entire width of the lane, carrying paper boats towards Kakoo's open gutter round the bend.

Facing the table in the corner is a shelf full of books belonging to Father. They are all in English. Hamisi says that Father read a lot once, even more than I do, before they married him off to Mother and that after marriage he gave up reading books altogether. I am not so sure. I have seen Father stand before the shelf, looking long into an open book, then close it with a nod and return it to the shelf, his right hand caressing the spine as if reluctant to leave it. If he knows where to open the book, he must also have read it before. That may well be, Hamisi counters, but have I, he asks, ever seen Father sit down to read a book the way I do, with the dictionary by my side? In any case, Father's old zeal for buying books remains unabated. Once every few months, when Father comes to know about a new shipment, he goes to his friend Kitabwalla's bookshop instead of the mosque or his club for playing at cards, returning late with two, sometimes three, books. Does he buy them for me? For me to read when I grow up? Did he, when young, understand everything he read? He says I am lucky that the school has a library. He made a special plea to Master Desai, the class teacher in my new school, to lend me two storybooks a month instead of the statutory one.

Strange that Father should have given up reading books, almost totally. And so long ago. Even before he married Mother. That is why Mother says she does not know when Father stopped reading. Grandma should know. Father had just turned sixteen, Grandma thinks she remembers. That was shortly after Mother's family agreed to accept Father as their future son-in-law. They came to the house to agree on the wedding date. Grandma decided on pistachio sherbet followed by thick black coffee and almond *halwa*. Sodawalla delivered, late as usual, a huge cube of ice covered in gunny cloth to keep it from melting. Grandma asked Hamisi to break up the ice for sherbet. They were all seated in the shop with freshly laundered cushion covers for Grandma's stool and the chair by the concertina desk. That is when, Grandma says, they heard an eerie shriek from the farthest room. Grandma rushed in, leaving the guests to Grandfather's care. She saw Hamisi, frozen in a squat by the ice cube, hammer in right hand, chisel in left, unblinking eyes turned towards Father who was raving from his armchair, the fat volume of *Thousand and One Nights* on his knees. "They should have called you idiot, *Mjinga*, and not Hamisi," she heard Father holler. "Can't you get it into your head that ice will melt the glass?" Grandma, and Mama Ayah who had followed her, knew at once that what they had heard had nothing to do with *Ghar Dhani*. In the excitement of the preparations for the future in-laws' visit, they had forgotten about Father who spent the whole day on his own in the far room without food or drink, absorbed in the fairy tales of the Arab world. Grandma left Father and Hamisi with Mama Ayah and returned to the guests. She told them Hamisi had hit his thumb with the hammer and had gone berserk with pain. Mama Ayah pacified Father with a prayer, led him to the third-floor bedroom, gave him a cup of hot milk mixed with saffron and nutmeg and left him with his book, locking the door as she left. That was when and how my grandparents came to tell Father that if they were to get him a wife and that if he were to be allowed to join Grandfather in running the shop, he would have to start concentrating on his wife and on Grandfather's business and either give up reading altogether or reduce it a hundredfold.

I take down the abridged version of Defoe's *Robinson Crusoe* from the bookshelf, Father's coverless dictionary by my side. Sometimes I have to check the meaning of almost every other word. Some of these words are so rare or difficult they are not even in the dictionary. Often the meaning is given in words which themselves have also to be looked up. *Lah*. How many words can there be? I think of them existing outside the dictionary, floating. Some have a special sound, like the flapping wings of the flying horse, and I see them form into the shape of a carriage with Grandma in it. The carriage rises higher and higher and every time Grandma casts out a word, I run to catch and prise it open for meaning. Nobody knows what I am up to with the books. Perhaps *Ghar Dhani* does, because some ghosts can read minds. In which case, *Ghar Dhani* must be the only one who knows that when I decide to look at the two half-doors of the main entrance from the outside instead of the inside, I turn female left into male right. Maybe sister Faiza is a fibber and *Ghar Dhani* is a creature she has dreamed up.

I sit on the threshold separating the open verandah from the middle room. I have one of the six exercise books Grandma gave me. Hamisi comes to see me before sunset in his muslin *khanzu*, spotless. A white cloth cap covers his head, a mark of respect, I think, for his new teacher. I have decided not to begin with the alphabet, the way Master Rathod taught at the junior school. Instead I start the way Uncle Emarem did with my first English lesson. I write the letter *H*, then the letter *A*, followed by *M* ... getting Hamisi to repeat the sounds after me. "*huh* and *aa*, *HA*, *mm* and *ee*, *MI*, *ss* and *ee*, *SI*. Hamisi."

Hamisi's stubby fingers tremble across the letters. He looks up at me, then looks at the letters again, pronouncing each syllable in a low vibrant voice. "*Ha ... mi ... si*." Eyes still on the letters, Hamisi murmurs, "The first time. The first time I am written."

I look up and recognize the thrill in his eyes.

"Now you write it, Hamisi."

He adjusts his cap, wets the pencil tip with his tongue the way Father does, and with "*Bismillah*, In the name of Allah," begins to write.

"There, Nuri. I have done it." His dry fingers scratch across the word again. He stares long and still at what he has written, then looks up, grinning. "Give me another word, teacher."

I write *S* and *E* and *N* and *T* and get Hamisi to repeat the sounds after me, "*ss* for *S*, *eh* for *E*, *nn* for *N* and *tuh* for *T* and you already know *ee* for I."

"*Senti*," he reads aloud. "So that is what 'cent' looks like when written."

"You have two words now, Hamisi."

"And eight sounds. Another word, Nuri."

"Don't be in a hurry, Hamisi. You have to remember all these sounds and letters."

"Don't worry, Nuri, I won't complain of indigestion. Give us an English word now."

"No, Hamisi. Not until you have learned all the sounds of all the letters."

"How many sounds are there?"

"In English, there are twenty-six letters. But English is different. Kiswahili letters and words sound the way they are written, not like English."

"What?"

"Sometimes the same English letter has a different sound. Here, look at this letter *C*."

I write "CENT."

"*C* has the sound of ss as in 'cent' which is '*senti*' in Kiswahili. But it has the sound of *K* as in 'car.'" I write down "CAR," pronouncing *kk, aa, rr*.

"Why?"

"That is how the English speak."

"Hah, I should have guessed."

"What, Hamisi?"

"Don't you see? Even in their writing, they are never what they appear to be."

The next day, Hamisi says, "This is not difficult, Nuri. All a matter of sounds. Look at what I have written with the sounds you taught me." Hamisi turns to a page in the exercise book.

MAMA, *mother*
SISI, *us*
SASA, *now*
SIMAMA, *stand*

"And now, the best part, Nuri, my teacher." He turns to the last page in the exercise book and shows me scrawled in large letters covering the whole page, ASANTE, *thank you*.

Six months on and Hamisi can read and write Kiswahili and a little English. Everyone in the house is proud of him. Father sends him on errands delivering invoices with customers' names and addresses written in English. One day we learn that Father has found him a job with the Standard Bank. He breaks the news to the family because Hamisi cannot bring himself to tell us. If we have Hamisi's welfare at heart, Father says, we should let him go. "What, delivering letters for a bank?" Grandma cries. And Father says that Hamisi can now read and write and that the new job is only a first step. The day Hamisi leaves, Grandma goes to her bed and cries. I go up to the third floor alone and refuse to say good-bye to him. And on many afternoons after that day, I go to the third floor with my rosary, each bead a prayer that he should do well, even though I want him to return.

Grandfather has also changed. One day I heard him say to Grandma, "You must not worry, Gulu's mother. Hamisi will go far, I know. He is intelligent." And as she looked up, I thought she smiled. But I know Grandma grieves in silence. When I raised her face with both my hands under her chin, I saw how her cheeks had sunk deep into her toothless mouth.

On Hamisi's first visit, I sit in the shop with Grandma. She has asked Mother and Mama Ayah to make *biryani* and sweet vermicelli in coconut cream and pack some for Hamisi. She waits and fidgets. Hamisi comes, takes her right hand into his and kisses it. She returns the kiss on his hand and offers him the chair on which Father's customers usually sit. She asks how he likes his new job. He nods, says he is content. She does not ask him about what he has to do. She knows all about his new job. She tells him he is welcome to return any time he wants to. He thanks her. We sit in silence for a long time. When he gets up, he again takes Grandma's right hand into his and kisses it. Grandma kisses his hand in turn.

As months go by, Hamisi's visits to our house become less frequent. One day Father tells Grandma that Hamisi has been promoted. She smiles, lowers her head and mutters a prayer. Another day Father tells her that Hamisi has made headlines in the *Zanzibar Voice* for his speech criticizing the British and the Arabs. She frowns, shakes her head, then lowers it and mutters a longer prayer. She turns to me and says, "Our loss is Hamisi's gain. You have done what pleases Allah." Then she starts a chant from the first revelation to the Prophet through Angel Gabriel, "Read ... for thy Lord is the Most Munificent who teaches by the pen, teaches man that which he knew not ..."

"'Knew' is past tense of 'know'?" I remember Hamisi asking, sitting on the threshold that separates the open verandah from the middle room on the third floor.

"Yes, Hamisi."

"English speech comes from the mouth and not from the heart, I tell you. Take this word 'know.' The letter *K* has no sound and what follows has a sound different from the word 'now.'"

We laugh.

"And yet our language is not unlike theirs. In some ways at any rate. Our word '*upinduzi*' comes from '*pindua*.' And the same word in English, 'revolution,' must come from their 'revolve.' But, you know Nuri, our '*upinduzi*' has a better sound, don't you think?"

"Yes, Hamisi, '*upinduzi*' has a zing to it."

"Talking about the word 'know,' I want to know, Nuri, my teacher, what the wise English sheikh has written."

"What sheikh?"

"Sheikh Peer."

"You mean Shakespeare, Hamisi. He is impossible, Hamisi. Father has his complete works and I understand none of it."

"Why?"

"Too many difficult words."

"In that case, Nuri, we will both have to be patient and one day we will read this Sheikhpeare together."

"Shakespeare, Hamisi."

Years later in England where I am reading English at the University of London, I think of Hamisi and what he said about English being "in-tense." *Knew*, past tense. *Know*, present tense. *Now*, the present. My present, a darkened London apartment, letter in hand, looking out the window from my springless chair, oblivious to the drizzly gloom outside. *Now*, in the present, remembering, creating a new past. Now, the invasive present. *Upinduzi.*

The letter is from sister Faiza. She reminds me of the message Mother managed to send out of Zanzibar, that they were safe and that I was not to return before completing my studies. She writes of the terror, of the massacres, of the uncertainty, of the days spent in the scorching open camp without food or water, of children crying, of not knowing, of the spent force of their hopes like the blurred prayers of Bablo's paper charm.

Attached to the letter is a note, in a different hand. She says the bearer of the note was a barefooted soldier with a gun slung round his shoulder. He said he had been sent by his immediate revolutionary leader. The note came with some food, a few bananas and drinking water they shared with the children in their area of the camp. The note, in English, was addressed to Mother:

> *Salaams to Mother. Nuri's grandmother took me in, may she rest in peace. Her grandchild Nuri, your son, taught me to read and write. My salaams to him when you write. Please accept this little offering, all I can do for now. Hamisi.*

Guarantee of the Seal

Bablo and I go back a long way and I look forward to his annual visit to Calgary from Vancouver where he teaches physics. We spend the night over gallons of black coffee and home-delivered pizzas, and I see him off the following morning to one of his conferences in New York or Paris or Oxford. We argue all night long about our past, though we like to think of it as reminiscing. Shortly after midnight, I begin to feel that arguing with Bablo is more pleasurable in anticipation than in the actual experience of it. The feeling gets stronger as the night wears on, but I seem to forget this little truth over the months that follow, and by the time the brief prairie summer is upon us again, I start looking forward to his visit.

We go over the same ground every year, and in the same order. The ritual begins with Bablo preceding me into my study and plonking himself down into my swivel chair by the desk. I take the guest armchair by the door facing him and wait for him to turn round for a meditative look at the bookshelves lining the two walls. An exchange of a few words on my latest acquisitions, a grunt or two of approval from him, and we enter the fray.

The starting point is always our grandfathers who were cousins in the extended East Indian sense in which any relation of about the same age, however distant, is a cousin. They both left

India in the last quarter of the nineteenth century to settle in Zanzibar. Tonight we ease ourselves into the argument by speculating on the perils of the monsoon-driven dhow journey across the Indian Ocean. The journey must have taken several weeks, we assume, and must often have been hazardous. Did not a cousin of our grandparents drown on his way back to India to find himself a wife? How did they cope with downpours at night as they lay on open decks? And how did they manage their toilet, squatting over the hole in the swinging wooden platform jutting out of the dhow, exposed to the elements and in full view of the crew and passengers? Did female passengers have to endure the same exposure? Our curiosity about such matters, never strong enough to goad us into research, soon gives way to the first of our skirmishes: over the motives that led our grandparents to leave India.

"For a better life," I suggest.

"To make money," he counters. "Typical *dukawalla* mentality."

Absurd distortion, I think, but say, "They were not shopkeepers when they came to Zanzibar; they were penniless farm workers."

"Exactly. From Indian rags to *dukawalla* riches. That about sums up our history."

Outrageously sweeping, I feel, coming particularly from an academic, making *khitchdi*-mush of our history. "You have obviously swallowed the drivel of your colonial masters," I say. "Like Uncle Mzungu."

"How, but *how* can you speak about me in the same breath as that, that …" he splutters.

The rush of red to his walnut-brown face. Have I hit below the belt? Am I being unfair in comparing him with the East Indian civil servant we called Mzungu, "European" because he was "London educated," by virtue of what we discovered much later to be a three-month tour of municipalities in Scotland? He certainly played a pivotal role in our parents' decision to send us to British instead of Indian universities. Left hand pointing east in the direction of India and a booming nasal accent we took to be British, he said to the gathering of our two families convened specially to seek his advice, "*Arre*, they will become more like Indians over there." Shaking his head with a vigour strenuous enough to dislocate the neck of a lesser person, he cried, "No, no, no, *no*, my dear sirs and madams." Right hand now stabbing in the direction of the northwest: "For real brass polish, you have got to send them home to England." How modern and British he looked, pausing for effect, caressing his luxuriant handlebar moustache, his unblinking eyes surveying first the elders seated on cane chairs and then the children cross-legged on the linoleum floor. Yes, a towering figure rising from shiny black shoes all the way up via white knee-length socks, perfectly creased white shorts, gleaming white shirt and, beyond the imposing moustache, the bushy eyebrows above bright bulbous eyes.

Bablo's face does not take long to assume its normal brown. "Hah," he cries. "Typical slave mentality, that Mzungu's, aping his colonial masters."

"What a contrast," I retort, "between the devastating clarity with which we notice deficiencies in others and the total blindness to the same deficiencies within ourselves."

Bablo stares at me.

"Did we not as students in Britain work on our accents, aping the public school types, to impress, to be accepted in the same way we accuse the Mzungu of doing? And with what result? An accent not quite BBC nor quite East African Indian, but, I suppose, acceptably educated, whatever that means?"

"Exactly what I am driving at, Nuri, don't you see? At the root of it all is the fact that we are cowards and it is this cowardice that manifests itself in our behaviour."

It is my turn to stare at him.

"Why do you think that, after graduation, we did not return and fight against second-class brown citizenship in East Africa, *hehn?*" he asks, pauses a second, then answers, "*Dukawalla* cowardice." In a rising voice, "Why do you think we decided to join the cultural mosaic in Canada instead of remaining, in perpetuity, coloured immigrants in England, hehn?" He bows and answers with a wide sweep of his right arm, "*Dukawalla* prejudice again." In a continuing crescendo, "And not a squeak from either of us when Enoch Powell thundered about the Roman seeing the River Tiber foaming with blood or when they screamed about the country being swamped with alien hordes. What did we –"

"Whoa, man, hang on a minute," I interrupt. "Has it ever occurred to you that practical prudence might have been the guiding principle as much for our forebears as for us?"

"Hah, what a weasel word, or rather, phrase. Are we now to cover up our cowardice with a veneer of practical prudence?"

Bablo seems shaken, perhaps ashamed that he got carried away. Head lowered, arms folded across his chest, he grimaces, then looks up grinning and asks, quite irrelevantly, "Do you remember Mrs. Iensen?"

I did indeed remember Mrs. Iensen, a guest we had met at a wedding reception in Copenhagen last spring. When she insisted on knowing where we were *really* from, we decided not to allow her the comfort of the facile belief that we were not Canadian. No, we were not aboriginals. Yes, we were *really* Canadian. No, we were not born in Canada, we were born in East Africa. No, we were not African, no longer that is. Yes, our grandfathers but not our grandmothers were from India. And finally, our stupefaction at her triumphant "Aha, I knew all along you were really Indian."

"You see, Nuri, it seems not only the Iensens of this world don't know who we are. Even we don't know."

He pauses for some sort of response. I do not oblige.

"What are we, Nuri?" His voice now raised in readiness to resume battle. "Kutchi, Zanzibari, British, Canadian, Indian? Each or some or none of these?" He shakes his head. "What a bloody cock-up, producing cocktails like us."

He leans across the desk. "Mongrel," he growls, more by way of an accusation than argument. I continue watching him without replying.

"That's what you, er, we are. Mongrels," his voice pitched higher, chin jutting forward in the manner of a challenge going back to our childhood – only this time, not to brave evil spirits in the cemetery without protective charms tied round our arms or wake the night watchman and run to avoid capture and a beating.

"I prefer to think of myself as a chameleon, at home in any society I happen to be in," I say, not wishing to rise to the bait.

"Hah. So many colours you don't know what your true colour is," he sneers, then lowers his head again. Mrs. Iensen is the wound he touches every so often to remind himself it still hurts.

"Yes, chameleon is just right, Nuri. But you know what is at the bottom of it all, don't you? Call it colour, ethnicity, visibility, race. Call it what you will – that is the one thing which has guaranteed our remaining inhibited outsiders, wherever we have lived."

"Huh, that is probably because we have never been to a country where everyone is brown," I offer without thinking and am immediately struck by my statement.

Bablo stops swivelling. His unseeing eyes narrow on Achebe's *Things Fall Apart* in the bookshelf to the left. Elbows on armrests, fingers tapping nostrils, his forehead wrinkles in thought. I feel as if I have unearthed a deeply buried truth. When we begin again, we find ourselves talking about preparations for a holiday in India.

We decide on a winter visit. Most of India is at its best then, Bablo says. He suggests three weeks, which is also about the maximum I can take from my work at the local library. Not long enough, we agree, but we do not have to spend more than a few days in New Delhi, with a day trip to the Taj Mahal. A stop or two in Rajasthan and the rest of the time in Gujarat with Ahmedabad as our starting point. We realize that we might have to decide on a base in Kutch to allow forays into villages in the area where our grandparents came from. Bablo takes it upon himself to make travel arrangements, and I agree in advance to accept whatever itinerary he decides on. I do not want to read anything on India. My first visit to India is to be uncontaminated by facts.

"And we have got to look like them," Bablo says.

"We already do."

"Don't be daft. With our t-shirts, pants and sneakers, they will be able to tell at once we are not of them. No, Nuri, we will have to buy our clothes in India when we land."

"Why do we always have to be other than who we are, Bablo? For once, why can't we just *be* ourselves? India became free twenty-three years ago, yet we are still in chains of our own making."

"But we *are* different, Nuri," Bablo says, his voice now subdued, almost gentle. "Why do we also have to *look* different when we can quietly merge with them?"

I am not persuaded but decide not to argue. I try to think how I would look dressed as an *Indian* Indian, and soon realize that Indian dress varies with region and perhaps caste or religion and, in large cosmopolitan cities at any rate, we could go about without anyone bothering or even noticing that we are visitors.

"And, at least in small towns and villages, we should not speak in English."

"But that is the only language we are good at, Bablo. Our Kutchi is more like pidgin than a language proper."

"I know, Nuri, but the Gujarati we learned at school is not that bad. With so many ethnic groups there, we would pass as visitors from another part of India wherever we happen to be. Yes, we should speak Gujarati, and not our Zanzibari pidgin."

New Delhi. We enter the hotel room. Bablo goes into the washroom to check if it is clean and if the toilet flushes. Feels the towels, sniffs. Lifts the bed sheets, sniffs. I already know he will repeat the performance in every hotel we stay at. For our first breakfast in India I ask for *masala paratha* and all the chutneys and pickles on offer at the hotel. Bablo sticks to tea and toast.

Bablo reminds me that our first task is to get "Indian" clothes. The hotel manager recommends a clothier. Our way lies through the chaos that is the Old City. Something vaguely familiar about the claustrophobic lanes. The piercing pitiful eyes of poverty. And the smell, a mixture of gas, urine, burnt cow dung, sweat. We have

been here before, I feel, albeit vicariously, perhaps in our childhood, through the press of poverty we did not notice in the narrow
lanes of Zanzibar. Perhaps if we stay in India long enough, we will
cease to notice it here as well. The few remarks I make to Bablo
elicit grunts. We walk on in silence.

The clothier turns out to be a Shah who greets us in Gujarati
as if he knows who we are. His gesticulating welcome includes an
immediate order for two *pyalas* of masala chai before we even sit
down. Bablo, visibly alarmed, suggests bottled mineral water
instead, a correction immediately barked out at the barefooted
boy servant leaving the store. "Loose-fitting shirts and pyjama
pants. Yes, sirs, just right, just right for this country." For someone
with such an enormous girth, he is startlingly agile in climbing
up the shelves. He knows exactly what to look for and where,
throwing down ten pairs of shirts and pants and, as he descends,
assuring us that each single one of them is "guaranteed." He does
not agree with our choice of colour, white, pointing out problems
of frequent washing, but Bablo's irritated repetitions of "*Nai, nai,
nai*" bring the Shah round to accepting white as "Excellent choice,
sirs, excellent choice, for this climate." Bablo refuses to haggle. He
looks sullen when I begin the pleasurable to-and-fro on the price
with the Shah. Anyone born and brought up in Zanzibar, I tell
Bablo later, knows that a good shopper haggles and that
dukawallas suspect non-hagglers of being either wimps or
foreigners. "And what did you achieve, Nuri? All that time and all
that effort and the result is a reduction in price by the equivalent
of one Canadian dollar." I shut up.

We go back to the hotel, change into our loose shirts and pants
and go out for a trip on the local sightseeing bus. Bablo suggests
we sit separately so that each of us gets a seat by the window. He
shares his window seat with a small man wearing a large red
turban which dwarfs a wrinkled face. The paan-chewing
neighbour turns out to be adept at spitting straight past Bablo
and out the window. He declines, politely, Bablo's offer of
exchanging seats. Bablo is a guest in his country and should have

a window view, the good neighbour insists, oblivious of the
squirming guest's uncertainly about the timing of the next missile.

In Gujarat at last, birth place of our forebears, where everyone
speaks Gujarati or Hindi, where billboards and newspapers are in
Gujarati, where blaring from the stalls and shops and from the
loudspeakers of vans and trucks are Gujarati and Hindi movie
songs and *bhajans*, most of which we know, though without a
complete understanding of what the words mean.

One of the pleasures I have long looked forward to in Gujarat is
unrestrained culinary indulgence. I am prepared to try any dish
that looks remotely interesting and particularly if on offer is something I have not had for years, curried *guar* or *khitchdi* or a good
tamarind moist *bhel* full of chickpeas, daal *bhajias* and fresh *chevdo*
mix. What I have not counted on is Bablo's perverse objections to
eating anywhere not recommended by his travel books.

On our way to the port of Mandvi, I suggest we try the *puris*
being fried on the railway platform.

"Even you must admit no bacteria can survive all that frying,"
I say.

"But the damned *puris* have to be held in something, man," he
cries. "Look, just look at the filth on his pile of newspaper plates."

"Suppose we ask the vendor to give them to us direct from the
frying pan?"

"Will you never get it, Nuri? All those years of exile in the
West?"

"What are you talking about?"

"Immunity, man. We might have lost our childhood immunity."

Every suggestion for trying something new or interesting to
eat is unacceptable to Bablo even when the eating places are
suggested by the managers of hotels recommended by his own
wretched guide books. We are nearing a point, I feel, when even
a glance at the forbidden fruit in the bazaars will elicit the
crushing weight of his snort. Not that I do not understand his
concerns, some of which I even share, like avoiding unboiled or

unbottled water. "The seal is the guarantee," he once said severely. "Not even *they* can harm its contents." But there is a limit, I tell him again and again, to what he regards as rational behaviour.

The only concession is his willingness to visit the homes of the new acquaintances we make. The parents of the child who came running after us in the bazaar to return what he thought was a gold pen we had lost. The teacher who sat on our luggage dropped off by the bus conductor at an earlier stop until we came to retrieve it. The factory owner we shared the railway compartment with. But the warmth and hospitality of our hosts seem only to push him further into his stubborn rigidity. On the first occasion when a village school teacher invited us to his spotlessly clean house, albeit set in a filthy area, Bablo went uninvited into the kitchen to supervise the woman of the house, only to rush out drenched in tears from the smoky firewood. He accepts nothing but tea, made to his order, with milk heated to a boil. I decide that I ought to impress upon our hosts that not all Zanzibari Canadians of East Indian descent are to be judged by Bablo's behaviour. On each of these visits, therefore, I sit myself on the floor, cross-legged like my hosts, take large morsels of their offerings, slowly bring each to my mouth, and with a jerky swish suck it in for noisy mastication. On the last of these visits I succeed in rounding up the meal with a loud appreciative belch. The barely concealed horror in Bablo's eyes is exquisite.

As for our attempt at disguising ourselves as Indians in small towns and villages, I am afraid we have been total failures. To our bafflement, we can be identified by anyone without any hesitation for what we are – foreigners. Our polite inquiries for a satisfying explanation are no match for the even more polite and tactful answers.

"Is it the way we wear these clothes?"

"*Nai, nai, nai, bhai sahib.* You look most certainly all right in them," is the usually prompt head-shaking response.

"Is it the way we walk?"

"*Hai* Ram, there is nothing wrong in the way you walk. You are, how to put it, more observant as you walk." A clear reference to Bablo's circumspection about what he steps on, sometimes lingering over the object he has avoided.

"Perhaps it is our speech."

"*Arre*, your grammar is better than that of our modern-day youngsters."

"What is it then that gives us away?"

"Difficult to say, *bhai*. You look, er, different."

It seems we are Indians everywhere in the world except India.

The night before our visit to our grandparents' birthplace, we sit up in his hotel room discussing how or why we look different.

"Do you remember the teacher's wife, what she said?"

"No, Nuri."

"That we were gentle, more like polite."

"What did she mean?"

"Not sure. Perhaps the same as what Soniji said in the railway compartment we shared with him and again what his wife said later at their home."

"What?"

"That we often say 'Thank you' and 'May I have?' instead of 'I want.' And we are liberal with our 'thank yous' and 'sorrys.'"

"Hm."

For a while we sit in silence. He seems exhausted, his face lowered in his hands.

"Are you disappointed you are not Indian?" I ask on an impulse, not entirely sure what I am about.

He looks up, says nothing.

"You seem to go out of your way to distance yourself from others."

He continues giving me his uncomprehending look.

"And such distancing from them seems to reflect your distancing from, not accepting, your own self."

"My several selves," he smiles. "So much for this … this pilgrimage to India. To discover ourselves." He nods, then murmurs as if to himself: "Acceptance." He nods again.

We get up before sunrise. Bablo complains of mild diarrhea and slight temperature but feels well enough to travel by bus. We follow a ten-year-old meandering behind a cow, pail in hand, ready to receive a deposit. All the way, Bablo's frowned concentration focuses on nuggets on the streets. Through the chaos of the narrow bazaar with cardamom turmeric asafetida sandalwood sulphur soap-nuts green and yellow and purple pistachios fat white cashew herbs and spices and nuts of the entire Eastern Hemisphere spiralling in one huge exhilarating waft. And all the way through the fruit and vegetable market, human beings every square inch, in shades of brown light brown dark brown almond brown walnut brown, men in *dhotis* pants shorts, women in *saris purdhas shalwar khameez*, children in brown black white sandals shoes barefoot naked, all jostling shouting haggling *two rupees, get that goat out, none better, from Madras, feel it, feel it, see the seal, brother, guaranteed seal, fresh brinjal, arre you can smell the colour, aiii papaya.*

We arrive early at the bus stop. With the cheery paan spitter still fresh in mind, Bablo insists we go all out for a double seat. The queue dissolves into a scramble for places before the bus comes to a stop. Bablo covers his head with a cotton scarf as protection against liquid missiles and plunges in, head first. I allow myself to be propelled in by the unyielding mass, arriving in time to jump into the empty space next to Bablo. The driver leaves for his cup of chai, the conductor goes up on the bus roof to tie up luggage, and the passengers open their tins and layered tiffin sections to fill the still air with the spiced smells of *chevda, bhel, pakodas* and *barfi*. I exchange a *penda* with a Kutchi passenger for one of my Canadian chocolates under Bablo's somewhat softened glare. The driver returns. The conductor whacks the side of the bus as a signal and the journey begins, dispersing the spiced smells.

As we enter a treeless terrain, Gujarati-Kutchi-Hindi chatters subside into silence.

About an hour and a half into the barrenness, the bus comes to a sudden halt. The engine or the gear box, nobody seems sure. The driver and the conductor decide to walk back for help to the village we left behind, about an hour's walk. "Why did they both have to go?" Bablo grumbles. The response is the shaking of many heads in unison.

"How far is the next village?"

"One mile."

"*Arre, nai, nai, bhaisaheb.* Three miles at least."

"Too far in this heat."

"But they are used to it from where they come."

"Where do you come from?"

"Europe?"

"*Arre,* I heard them talk. Sounded Amreecan."

"Where do you come from, *bhai?*"

"Canada."

"I told you."

We conclude the next village cannot be more than an hour away on foot. We decide to walk ahead, expecting to be picked up by the bus on arrival.

The dry heat soon begins to take its toll on us. Bablo gets paler by the step. There are no trees for shade, only desert bushes. We stop every fifteen minutes for rest, then walk on in silence. Bablo has difficulty breathing. Not like him not to carry his bottled water. I begin to worry about dehydration. After almost an hour on the road, we see a distant object silhouetted in the vibrant haze. The structure materializes into a hut as we approach. The village consists of just this one dwelling, its front converted into a store, a convenient stop for the rare bus that passes by. Black flies rise as one thick black sheet at being disturbed, revealing the moist brightness of sweetmeats, mostly *jalebi.* The owner, an old man, is under five feet. Slender. He wears a toothbrush moustache and looks like Charlie Chaplin, except that his face is leathery and wrinkled and his shiny eyes lie distant in their sockets. I feel he knows we are not Indian. He helps Bablo to his chair in the shaded part of the store. I begin scanning the shelves. Nothing drinkable in sight. The owner offers tea. Bablo shakes his head. How about sugar cane juice, freshly crushed only that morning? Bablo shakes his head again. Water? No, thank you.

A gentle breeze stirs the stillness. I look up at something flapping against the wall. A yellowed map of India above the shelf. A cola bottle lies horizontally on the highest shelf, half in the sun, half covered by the map. I get up. The bottle feels warm. It has the guarantee of the seal. "Untouched, uncontaminated by humans," as my companion has often insisted. "Thanks," he whispers as I give it to him. He turns it in his hand, his pale face betraying no emotion. He looks at the owner and passes the bottle on to his stretched hands. The old man takes a nearby opener, prizes off the top. He hesitates, looks into the bottle, shoves his right forefinger inside, clears the neck, takes his finger out with a loud pop, smiles as he returns it to Bablo. The entire operation takes the old man a fraction of a moment, his rapid movement Chaplinesque in jerkiness, finishing before we can protest.

Bablo stares at the bottle, his mouth open. I look at the old man who is grinning at him. I turn to Bablo and begin to feel I must have been hit by the sun because he appears flat against a depth-less background, as in the Moghul paintings we saw in New Delhi. His tired face widens into an unfamiliar grin and there is a return of brightness to his eyes. He stands up, as if in slow motion, cola bottle in hand. He stays motionless for an eternity. His movements, when they begin, continue in slow motion. He puts the bottle to his mouth and empties the contents in three exquisite gulps. With a loud belch, he walks towards me. "There are no certain answers," he whimpers. "Not even the seal is a guarantee."

Mother

Something about Mother's latest letter fills me with a particular sense of foreboding. It is written, as ever, in her even, bold hand and addressed to her three children: the original for the eldest, and photocopies for the other two. I initially notice no change in the structure of her prose – preliminaries of prayers for our health, wealth and spiritual progress, in that order, followed by the dates of her triennial visit to each of us. Attached to each copy, always, is a much longer PS with individual advice and instructions. For me, this time, my PS includes an easy two-minute bachelor recipe for *brinjal* curry she has perfected and which she wants me to try out and report back on. I read the letter again, taking my time, even with the preliminaries. She will visit first "my eldest, Sham, now settled happily in England with his good wife, Leila." Then she will visit "dear Faiza, happily settled in Texas with her good husband Shiraz and my only dearest grandchild, Liyana." Last of all she will come to see me, "my youngest and dearest Nuri in Canada." Innocuous enough, I think. I think again. She has never written or spoken of my siblings as *settled* with their *good* spouses. The subtext, clearly meant for me, is alarming.

The whole family knows what she means by "settled." Her favourite tautology is: "You are not settled until you are married."

113

That is why – I can see her saying as she adjusts her white silk *sari* before the long mirror on the first floor of our house in Zanzibar – she felt duty-bound as mother to help my brother and sister choose their partners. And a "good" spouse is one who comes from a respectable Zanzibari family, though the convoluted ways in which she determines respectability and connection to Zanzibar are outrageously flexible. A Rwandan-born grandson of a man who used Zanzibar as a staging-post for supplies in the late 1800s before moving on to the interior of Africa may qualify while the "foreign-born" son or daughter of someone born in Zanzibar may not. Even my sister's good husband, born and bred in Texas, has given up trying to unravel the intricacies of his connection with a 1930s Zanzibar so triumphantly established by Mother.

With both my siblings settled, I have to brace myself for the imminent concentration of her inexhaustible energy on her only remaining target. Yet whenever I think of Mother as an unreasonable and unreasoning force, I feel I am deficient in understanding and am being mean. Persuading myself that most mothers are like her does somewhat assuage the gnawing feeling that I am in some way being ungrateful. At moments like this I switch to remembering her as a young woman, slim, sprightly, with long black hair tied into a bun during the daytime and let casually down in the evening, jasmine flowers woven through it all the way to her waist. Sometimes I imagine her the way Grandma must have seen her, as a young bride of fifteen coming into a household strange to her, to train under her formidable mother-in-law and to look after the extended family of ten. She is still slim and, for all her sixty-odd years, nimble on her feet, with discreet silver strands in her dyed dark-brown hair. I think of how her soft face lights up with an infectious smile whenever she sees someone she knows. And how her large dark eyes raised almost covertly at a stranger never fail to elicit a smile in response. Even as a child, she was as much a friend as a parent, someone to talk matters over with and to play with. And when I was caught committing misdemeanours, her punishment, a slap on the back, never hurt, though the words accompanying the smack were sufficient rebuke to keep me on the straight path until my next deviation. Moments of forgiveness after punishment were bliss, lolling in her lap as she sat on the linoleum floor, her hand crawling along my back, singing as if to herself a song of Radha longing for her Krishna.

I collect her from the airport. As I am about to start the car, I feel her hand extended in invitation to mine.

"Let me have a good look at you, *mwanangu*, my child." We sit in silence for a while, her eyes on me and my eyes on her warm hands clasping mine. We sit still, perhaps for a minute or two, and then, in a voice that is more like an order from the young Mother I remember, she says, patting my hand, "And you don't have to remind me how I should behave in your country."

We laugh, but the foreboding returns. She has never before referred to Canada as my country. I have always been a Zanzibarbarian to her. I am not sure what to make of her acknowledgement of me as a Canadian. Living in Canada must have changed me at least somewhat but not, I hope, in any way that goes to the core of my Zanzibari being. Whatever the explanation, I am surprised and happy to have her in my city again, though the feeling of guilt persists for having lectured her on her previous visits when I still lived in downtown Calgary: "Do not ask strangers if they are married. And their religion is their own private, very private affair. One more thing, never, ever, ask about their salary." My only consolation, I tell myself, is that there would have been no other way of curbing her overweening inquisitiveness. But she never argued, only nodded a silent assent to each of my strictures, intensifying each time the pang of undeserved guilt in my stomach. I suspect she learned this unsettling if not irritating habit from Grandfather, who also rarely argued back when Grandma was annoyed. I suppose, especially at his age, he was more than experienced and mature enough to know that once Grandma had made up her mind, nothing he said or did could make a difference.

Not that Mother operates in two modes only: nodding her
assent in silence or issuing a fatwa to be followed without question.
There are occasions, of her own choosing, when she argues, and
argues well – as when she reasons for acceptance of racial, ethnic
and cultural diversity as a matter of necessity for survival in an
increasingly pluralist world – and I have to admit to myself, with
somewhat reluctant pride, that she is blessed with wisdom. On
one of her previous visits, when I still lived in the downtown
apartment, I disagreed with her view that living in a city involved
the impoverishing loss of the sense and feel of community.

"You seem to be seeing through your own tinted lenses,
Mother," I heard myself say as she sat cross-legged in her favourite
wide armchair turning rosary beads in her hand.

"They are the only ones I have," she said, raising her hand,
reprimand in her eyes.

"Of course I belong to a community, or, rather, communities,"
I insisted. "The colleagues at work, the friends I play badminton
with, the communal prayers that I attend, albeit not as often as
you would like me to. They are all my community. None of us is
a Canadian *sadhu* living in the rugged wilderness of the Rockies."

"Tell me one thing, man of the world. Tell me about the
tenants who occupy this ghost town of an apartment you live in.
How many of them do you know? Take your next-door neighbour.
You probably don't even know if it is a he or a she. In Zanzibar, we
know."

"And interfere and gossip," I interrupted.

"Yes," she said, unaffected by what was meant as a barb. "There
is, of course, a price to pay, but the point I am making is that I, we,
know about one another and we care in a way that enriches us.
How can you care if you do not even know? How can there be
true compassion without knowledge? Is that not what I have
heard you complain about when you talk of the West's ignorance
concerning the eternally developing countries?"

During her past visits, when I still lived near Calgary Tower,
Mother had taken advantage of annoyingly limitless opportunities

for meeting strangers, giving free rein to her greed for useless information. "Are you married? How many children do you have? Grandchildren? What is your religion? Where do you live?" She has always been a complete stranger to the idea of privacy. The nearest she comes to grasping it is in the concept of isolation, and I certainly do not tell her that what she calls isolation is a shield protecting others from her predatory overtures. And yet, for some reason I have never been able to understand, Calgarians have always indulged her: in apartment corridors, on trains and buses, in restaurants, at barbeques. She seems to compel a response to her advances on her terms. Now that I live on an acreage in Bearspaw Ridge Village, I am relieved that opportunities to let herself loose on unsuspecting strangers will be limited. "But why do you call it 'village'?" she asks as we enter the acreage. "You have no shops, no gas stations, no churches, no coffee houses to meet at. Whose idea was it to call it a village?"

She elicits from me the details of my daily life. About my work as a librarian, am I happy? About my daily meals, what do I have for lunch at work? About the house, how often does the cleaner come and how much does she charge? About my spiritual health, how often do I meditate and for how long, do I say my daily prayers on time, how often do I attend communal prayers in the evenings? About the three-acre lawn, how long does it take to mow? My neighbours, why do I not visit them? About the winter, how do I cope with the cold?

I ask her, in turn, about Hamisi, our servant turned revolutionary politician, who spends most of his time abroad as an ambassador and who, on his visits to Zanzibar, comes to pay his respects to Mother. She tells me that Halima, the little girl I wanted to marry as a child, is happily married, with five grown children and three grandchildren. We talk about Uncle Emarem who taught me to read and write English and who never recovered from his bypass surgery in India and whose vast book collection was donated to the local library.

The question-and-answer sessions occur when we sit out in the garden during evenings of chinook warmth, watching the sun set behind the Rockies. The intervals between questions are long, and though she asks about very little that she does not already know, she seems to be at peace. I, too, am at peace.

She does not want me to take her out during the daytime to visit her friends or cousins, most of whom I see only during her visits to Calgary. They all seem happy to give her rides to and from their homes.

"But what of the days when you do not go out visiting?"

"Hah, child, you seem to forget that I am no longer young. Gallivanting around tires me and I need rest days."

I am not convinced.

"Don't you remember how much I love walking? What more of a blessing can I ask for than the two magnificent signs of Allah – the rugged Rockies and the prairie sky?"

The sparkle in her eyes is reassuring.

She has asked all her friends and acquaintances not to make calls in the evenings and weekends which are "reserved for my youngest son." The occasional phone calls she gets in the evenings are uncharacteristically brief. On one occasion, I am surprised to hear her speak in English over the phone, but decide that she was probably speaking to her friend's child who was brought up in Canada and was understandably without Kiswahili or Kutchi.

I look forward to returning home from work at the library and to be greeted by her "How did your day go?" She tells me about her visits to our relations or, on rest days, about her "bracing walk in your village." And then we sit down to delectable meals prepared with specially blended spices she brings with her from Zanzibar. She knows what my favourite dishes are: her succulent *biryani* and coconut chicken *paka*, her samosas in paper-thin crisp wrappers, and her best-ever puddings, floating mountain and creamy *kulfi*.

Once a week I take her out to see Old Bapa who was a friend of Grandma's and who has now come to live with his married son in Calgary. He is well versed in our devotional literature and she invariably spends the whole day with him. Her only regret, she tells me, is that she might not be able to see her old Zanzibari friend Alibhai who lives in High River. He is abroad visiting his daughter, a supervisor of a rehabilitation project in Tajikistan. She fears he might not be back before she returns to Zanzibar.

Mother has not yet raised the matter of helping me "settle." I am on guard. I know she can be devious, though I do not understand how my brother and sister could have failed to see through her as she went about deciding their partners for them. From past visits, I know her strategies. Perhaps she will invite to Bearspaw a Zanzibari woman she knows, with her daughter. All concerned know what the invitation is about – somewhat embarrassing, I complain, but have to admit that the entire proceedings are open, honest and honourable. Her less-open strategy involves asking me to drive home her friend, who, on reaching her house invites me in for tea, during which I meet the prospective bride. She has also dragged me to picnics, communally and privately arranged, and insisted that I take her twice a week to our evening prayer house, which is an excellent venue for seeing and being seen. For my escape from the matrimonial trap so far, some of the credit must go, ironically, to Mother herself, as she has, until now, been more concerned with the propriety of getting her eldest son married first. The rest of the credit must go to Providence. During a picnic arranged by Mother, the prospective girl had an attack of hay fever. On another occasion, the girl I was required to go out with on a short walk after lunch lost no time in telling me that she already had a white, Christian, Canadian boyfriend, that her parents did not approve of their relationship, and that I would understand if she did not particularly want to sound encouraging. I was not quite sure how to take this rejection, but looked forward to telling Mother of the lapse in her investigative prowess, only to discover that she already knew.

The six weeks of her visit are nearly over. She leaves for Zanzibar tomorrow morning. A depressing feeling of guilt looms over me. I have misjudged her. Not once has she embarrassed me in Bearspaw Ridge Village with her overtures to strangers. Not once has she raised the question of marriage or arranged for me to meet a girl. I feel I have been uncharitable. Perhaps she has given up on me. It could be that she still has a card up her sleeve, but what her strategy could be escapes me. At night we talk for the last time about the past. About Father who died shortly after the Revolution, all our property taken over by the new government, about Grandfather and Grandma and about Mama Ayah who saw most of us through childhood. I insist she come to Calgary every year but she says she is getting on and that I should visit her at least once every two years. She does not once express the hope and prayer, as she always has in the past, of welcoming me to Zanzibar with my bride. I believe she has at last accepted that her youngest son will get married to a woman of his own choice, in his own time and in his own Canadian way.

I drop her at the airport. She goes to the check-in while I drive on to park the car. When I return, I see her surrounded by a crowd. My first reaction is panic but I soon realize that the faces surrounding her are the familiar ones of friends and family, including about twenty less-familiar faces from Bearspaw Ridge Village. They see me approach. The elderly Mr. Blackburn who lives at the north end of the Village tells me what a privilege it is to know her and how lucky I am to have such a wise and compassionate woman as a mother. A young girl, whose name I cannot quite catch, tells me that Mother taught her to wear a *sari*. I begin to wonder how she could have come to know so many of my neighbours in so short a time when most of them are no more than familiar faces to me. I guess that she must have met at least some of them during the daytime walks she said she took when she was not visiting her Zanzibari friends. One such contact, I suppose, must have been more than enough for her to build a vast network of relationships in the Village. I discover that, in addition to her excellent Indian recipes, she has dispensed freely of her home-cooked wisdom on a bewildering variety of subjects: on indoor plants, on domestic tensions, on relaxation, on baby rash, on caring and, of course, on the same core of truth to be found in the esoteric writings of all their religions. She looks pleased and she knows I am pleased too. As she is about to leave for the security check, a tall girl, in her late twenties, comes running towards her. High cheekbones, shoulder-length black hair. "Just made it," I hear her whisper as Mother embraces her hard and long. She has a brief word with the girl, then she calls me.

"This is Nimira. She is like my second daughter," she says, stroking the girl's hair. "She came back from Tajikistan only last night."

"I must say again how sorry Father will be to have missed you," Nimira says, looking at Mother, and with genuine regret in her voice. Turning to me, she says, somewhat shyly I think, "He stayed on in England to be with a friend who is not well."

"Not to worry, Nimira," Mother says. "If Alibhai is still in England, phone him and tell him I am on my way. Tell him to contact me at my son's." Turning to me, she says, "You give her your brother Sham's address. And give her a ride back home."

Mother gives me a final long hug. I see tears in her eyes. I know I will miss her.

On the way back from the airport with Nimira, I discover that her brother and I went to the same school in Zanzibar, though he was several years my senior, and that she started at the same school as my sister and later, thanks to Mother's help in getting her a scholarship, she transferred to St. Joseph's Convent School. She tells me how Mother came into her own after the Revolution, organizing plumbing classes in Zanzibar for those who wanted to emigrate, and arranging scholarships for school graduates wishing to study in the West. I talk about myself and am surprised how easy it is for me to do so with this perfect stranger. I am glad she lives in High River, as the drive back to her home will be a long one. Our conversation ranges from the innocently personal

– our preferences in music and books – to a serious but civilized disagreement on the causes of the Revolution in Zanzibar. At her home, she invites me in for "a simple lunch" of curried chickpea soup she prepares in minutes, tangy, slightly chili hot and altogether delicious. We talk about Calgary and High River and about her project in Tajikistan. I leave late in the afternoon. She agrees to meet me for lunch at the Unguja Bistro this coming weekend. On the way back, a thought occurs to me about Mother, but I do not dwell on it. Other thoughts occupy my mind.

Trousers

The argument with Nimira started one night last winter. I was standing by her side, dishcloth in hand, ready for her to give me the *biryani* pot she was scouring with the steel pad.

"Your trousers have seen better days," she said without turning round. She spoke in a flat voice, with no hint of irritation or banter. I looked down at my trousers, more as a reflex than expecting to find a tear or a new blob of black. I answered with an equally matter-of-fact "hmm," as I do when she makes a casual remark about the weather or when she interrupts the ten o'clock news and says, almost in a trance, how contented our three-year-old Al looks sprawled out asleep on the floor.

Nimira had never before complained about or even commented on, except by way of approval in her eyes, what I wore. I thought no more of her remark until she raised the matter again early in the New Year. We were at the kitchen table sorting out Xmas cards from friends we had to send replies to.

"So what do you think?" she asked.

"About what?"

"Your trousers," she said, raising her voice a little as if I ought to have known what she meant.

"What about the trousers?"

"Get rid of them."

"Still some wear in 'em, I think."

She looked down at the frayed ends of the legs.

"They are comfortable," I continued.

She gave a dismissive grunt.

"And they have a familiar feel about them that … that exudes warmth."

"Reek, you mean," she corrected, looking up.

"I have grown into them."

"More like they have grown into you," she laughed. "Just look at them. They have even assumed your shape."

"But I feel at home in them."

"I should think so, Nuri. You have been living in them for years."

I realized then that I would have to wait for another day when she might be more receptive. That should also give me time to think of arguments she might find acceptable.

The occasion presented itself a few nights later. I had just put Al to bed when I came down to the kitchen. She was browsing through a catalogue with the pot of chamomile tea and two cups ready for me to join her at the table. She looked up. "He's fast asleep," I said and sat opposite her. She seemed relaxed.

"About the trousers," I began as she poured tea for us.

She looked up.

"They have sentimental value."

She closed the catalogue.

"They were part of the suit that Mother gave me on our engagement."

"I know."

"And I wore the suit at our wedding, do you remember, when we sat cross-legged on the floor of the prayer house to sign the marriage contract before the *mukhi*."

"Of course I remember, but don't you see, Nuri, what a punishing wear you have given them since?"

"They are not in tatters yet," I said.

"You remember what your mother had to say about them?"

"We can't take Mother's fixations seriously," I laughed.

I did not want to veer away from what I had intended. At the risk of sounding maudlin, I decided to come up with moments of happiness and sorrow I had shared with the trousers: when I had stood proud and erect in the citizenship court reciting with euphoric solemnity the Oath of Allegiance as she stood next to me; when I first felt Al's moist warmth in my arms; and again when I was awarded the Rotarian of the Year plaque by our local club. She did not interrupt and did not argue back. I knew then that I had got nowhere near explaining to her what I had intended: that the bond which existed between me and the trousers went beyond the merely physical. I had to admit to myself the futility of articulating what I could hardly understand myself, certainly not to Nimira, and most certainly not in the mood she was in.

In the days that followed, I wondered if Nimira's inflexibility was more than a matter of mood. The reasons she began to rely on increasingly seemed to have more to do with the state of her feelings than with the state of the trousers. She was even too ashamed, she said, to include them in the parcel of clothing she prepares every year for Zanzibar's Mituma Charity, of which she is the vice president. She was no longer prepared to endure the necessity of having to dismiss the subject by way of a joke when, quite incredibly, she began to think visitors to the house cast questioning glances at the wretched pair. And she seemed to have convinced herself that the trousers emitted an odour, indefinable but distinct, an odour to which, she complained, I was exasperatingly oblivious.

The strength of Nimira's feelings about something that she would normally dismiss with mock ridicule was so uncharacteristic of her that I felt I had to consider the possibility of Mother's hand behind the scene. I tried to recall what Mother had said during her past visits. I remembered her making a great fuss over an old pair of jeans of mine, but that had been a few years ago, and in any case I had just given up wearing them this year. They had been deemed good enough for inclusion among secondhand clothes Nimira stores in her wooden case in the basement awaiting its annual shipment to Zanzibar. I began to wish I had paid more attention to Mother's comments instead of dismissing them as based on ignorance of what is sartorially acceptable in Canada. I knew only too well that she could be devious, but I did not think Nimira would have taken seriously Mother's oft-repeated quip to her elderly friends that it is up to the woman of the house to keep her man on the straight and narrow.

I used to dread Mother's visits to Calgary. I no longer do. Back then, her obsessive object had been to get me married to a good Zanzibari girl. I am now married to such a girl. If Mother played any part beyond her introducing me to Nimira, I will never know. Both Nimira and I are happy she can visit us in spite of what must be an exhausting journey from Zanzibar. She has spent each of the last three summers with us in Calgary. "To be with my grandson Aleem," she coos, pronouncing the first syllable of her grandson's full name with guttural relish. She objects to our calling him Al and is quick to correct us even in the presence of others. I once made an unthinking remark about her insisting that we call the child by his full name when everyone else called him Al.

"So what is the problem?"

"Well," I began but could not immediately think of a reason.

"Do you think Aleem will grow up with uncertainty?"

"I suppose."

"A kind of uncertainty about his identity?"

As I nodded hesitantly, I knew that she was about to move in for her triumph.

"Hah, Nuri my child, fret not. Your son will then make a good Canadian."

Mother adores Al. For a woman who complains of advancing old age, Mother runs and bawls after her grandson, hauls him up high and catches him back breathless in a perfect hold, always has meals with him, and does not sleep until after he does. Nimira has seen her tiptoeing in the middle of the night for a peek and a nod at him. When Al is not well, Mother insists on her being his sole nurse, ordering whoever is about to bring her the little cloth bag she keeps under her bed, which is full of herbal powders and mixtures she always brings from Zanzibar.

I began to think that perhaps I might convince Nimira why comfort trumped fashion if I concentrated on arriving at a compromise. A new strategy was called for. I needed to put forward my arguments in the form of suggestions, and in a way that was neither irritating, which would turn her against me, nor smacked of near capitulation, which would make her suspicious of my intentions. I decided to raise the matter again when we went out for dinner one Tuesday, leaving our next-door neighbours Pete and Jenny to babysit Al.

"Let us meet halfway," I finally said in a spirit of compromise, as she picked up the last bit of *gulab jamun* on the dessert plate we had shared. I had decided not to pretend to sound mellow or regretful, for she would intuit that as posturing before I could even attempt a camouflage.

She smiled but said nothing.

"I want to keep the trousers and you don't." I realized even before finishing the sentence that I had stated the obvious. I was trying, unobtrusively, I hoped, to detect signs of conciliation in her, for I knew that once the shutters were down, even the gods would be barred entry into her mind.

She looked down at the empty plate, picked up the fork and put it down again.

"I don't think we should go into the reasons again, do you?"
She nodded.

"I never wear these trousers to work, you know that. Suppose I agree to wear them only when I go out into the garden."

A slight, almost imperceptible shake of her head made me feel I was getting nowhere.

"Not indoors," I persisted, "and ... and never, never when we go out."

Could a slight twitch in her right eye mean a willingness on her part to reconsider? In a firm tone, to convey I was in earnest, I blurted out my final concession for clinching the deal.

"And never when we are expecting visitors."

She looked up.

"This way we can accommodate both your public concern and my private comfort," I continued, immediately remembering her telling me once that there were times when I could sound pedantic.

Her eyes narrowed in thought as if she were suspecting a well-concealed loophole, which might yawn into an abyss at some future time of my choosing.

"All right, then," she began. Before I could take in the full impact of her words, she continued with the pursed-lipped stern-ness she usually reserves for admonishing Al, "But if you once, even once ... and you know what will happen to your precious trousers."

I wished then that we had been at home. I wanted to take her into my arms for a hug and a "love you" whisper in her ears. I stretched my hands for hers. She took them and gave them a gentle squeeze.

In the days that followed I thought again of Mother, feeling guilty for having suspected her of having had a hand in Nimira's sartorial resolve. But my immediate concern now was Nimira's skepticism. I could almost hear her thinking that the compromise would not last long, and that what had been agreed to between us was more of a cease-fire without any prospect of it ever maturing into a permanent peace. I resolved that I would have to prove her wrong.

Getting Nimira's agreement to a compromise, I soon began to realize, had been a mere flanking manoeuvre. The real battle lay elsewhere – within me. A Zanzibari *mwalimu* seemed to have cast a long-distance spell on me, so that any physical contact with the trousers brought on amnesia, but of a kind limited to my promise to Nimira. She was certainly no help. She did not complain about nor did she acknowledge instances of breach, which were unintentional and of which she must have known, like when I came in from the garden after a long day and was too tired to think of my trousers or anything else, and Jenny had come in to return a book and stayed on for tea. Like when I went straight from the garden to Pete's next door for a drink and an expert exchange of verbal notes on our newly planted shrubs. Like when she showed no sign of her good-natured revelling at my getting confused trying to reassemble the lawn mower I had so easily taken apart, and not having enough time to change into respectable clothes for a discussion on "Time Management" I had volunteered to lead at the Bearspaw Community Hall. As these instances of breach increased in frequency, she seemed to lose interest. I began to feel she had finally understood.

Two days ago Mother arrived for the summer. On Saturday, the day after her arrival, we arranged a barbeque for family and friends to welcome her. I spent the entire six hours in the offending trousers, without a thought about my many arguments with Nimira or my suspicion that Mother had had a hand in them. But then again, thinking over what happened this morning, I am not so sure that Mother was at all innocent in the matter. I cannot get rid of that feeling in the pit of my stomach. I know I am responsible for what Nimira must have had to endure at the barbeque. She probably had to ward off barbs, always oblique, aimed at her giving in too easily to her husband's well-worn arguments and at her total failure at getting him to mend his sartorial ways. Perhaps she had also to endure remarks, addressed to others but within her hearing, about what they do with rags in Zanzibar, or even to overhear yet again Mother's notions about the woman of the house having to keep her man on the straight and narrow. And all the while that day in the garden, I appeared to inhabit a world in which Nimira's concerns had no place – now racing with the children who had come, now sitting on the most comfortable garden chair with my legs stretched out, hands in pockets, now holding forth on the causes of the continuing tragedy in the Middle East.

Soon after breakfast this morning, Mother and Nimira went out to visit Old Bapa. I could not find my trousers. As I searched the house for them, I left Al in the sitting room to play at forcing letters into their slots of his alphabet board, coming in to keep an eye on him from time to time. They were not in the laundry bin or the washing machine, and they were not in Nimira's part of the wardrobe, which is supposed to be out of bounds for me for some reason I have never been able to fathom. I looked for them in cavities above the cupboards, in all the cabinet drawers, in the basement and even, inexplicably, in her small handbag she takes to the prayer house and in which, I know, she keeps only her rosary. I searched every nook and cranny I could think of. If she'd finally taken the matter into her own hands, I felt she could at least have warned me, though I realize now that prior notice would obviously have jeopardized her plan. I thought of Mother. I felt numb. I knew then that there was only one place left to look. I walked slowly to the garage and lifted the lid of the garbage bin. There they were. The once whole pair had been reduced to four pieces. What I felt was not anger, not surprise, not even sadness. Something of a void. I took out the remnants, put them into an empty bag with care, and returned them to the bin. I came back, looked in on Al and went down to the basement. Digging into the large wooden case of secondhand clothes Nimira stores for her Zanzibar charity, I took out the old pair of faded jeans I have not worn for nearly a year.

A Feeling of Unease

Every Sunday evening, between seven and eight, Nimira phones our son Al in Montreal. I get the first few minutes to exchange greetings with him, to ask if all is well with his studies at the university and if he needs anything. She then takes the handset from me and goes into the adjoining kitchen for her hour-long mother and son *tête-à-tête*. She says she wants to leave me undisturbed to catch up with the weekend newspapers. I spend the hour listening in on her part of the conversation instead. The topics usually covered fall under three headings: food, prayers and social life, in that order; and I can often predict her follow-up questions. Her "What did you have for breakfast today?" is, after allowing for his reply, followed by "Have you changed over to skim milk yet?" And "Did you attend Friday's communal prayers?" is often followed by "Did you meet anyone interesting?" I wait for her high-pitched expressions of displeasure in "How many times have I told you to keep away from fast foods?" or "What makes you think you can function with only six hours of sleep?" The part of the conversation I tend to wander off at concerns her commentary on the details of each dish he is served when he is invited out, though I admit to having picked up a few pointers during such exchanges: that it takes less than ten minutes to curry pigeon peas in coconut cream and that you can make *channa batata* without oil.

When the conversation is over, she returns to the sitting room, more to review her call than to fill me in, often interrupting her flow with "You will have to talk to him about sleep" or "I must send him a *daal* recipe which is so easy to make." Al seems to be more forthcoming with her. He must know that whatever he tells his mother filters through to me, though on occasions, when it suits them both, I suspect extensive editing en route, as when she got me to agree to buy him a new computer. To this day I have not been able to unravel how she did that. While I remember the different strands of the conversation, beginning with viruses and slowing of download speeds and moving on to new software and improvements in operating systems, I cannot see how she got them all together to make a case for a new machine.

Last Sunday's call was longer and deviated from the usual order of topics. Her voice often sank to a whisper and I found myself becoming irritated at not being able to make anything of her "What did she say?" or "Could it be that you are prejudiced?" or "What do they do?" When the call was over she burst into the sitting room, face flushed, and announced: "Al's got a girlfriend."

"Imagine, our Al's got a girlfriend," she repeated, glowing, as she dropped into the chair.

"Good for him," I said, lowering the newspaper I had been pretending to read.

"She's at McGill, too, and in the same year, and taking the same courses," she beamed. "Coincidence, you think?"

I assumed that she did not expect a reply.

"They are both organizing a Third World walk in Montreal." She paused, and then continued as if to herself: "They must be together a lot." Finally, turning to me, she said, "Her name's Sarah."

"What? You mean –"

"She is Chinese, Vancouver born and bred. Her parents are from Taiwan."

I stared at her. I found it difficult to accept that I could have been wrong all these years in believing that she wanted a daughter-in-law from our own ethnic community. Had she not always insisted that Al attend our prayer house regularly so as to meet others, meaning girls, of his age? And had she not said, more than once, how she hoped and prayed for a good bride for her son, one who would share our values? And had I not then laughed and said that she was as obsessive as Mother had been when it came to getting her son married? And here she was, rejoicing at the thought of a daughter-in-law who was not even East Indian, let alone from our own community.

"Sarah is eighteen," she continued. "Two months younger than our Al."

"And?"

"I asked him if he was in love and he just said he liked her. She is bright, he says. A good pianist. Has a wicked sense of humour. Oh yes, and she is very easy to get along with."

"What about her parents? What do they do?"

"They are retired. Their son has taken over the business. Something to do with real estate, but Al isn't sure."

"And how many siblings?"

"Just the brother."

"Are you brooding about Al again?" Nimira asks.

"No," I lie, without looking at her.

She gets up from her chair, grinning, joins me on the sofa and whispers, "Then why have you been staring at nothing these last ten minutes?"

And so we begin, as we have these past few nights, facing the turned-off TV screen. We know that after an hour or more we will be no further along from where we started. What began as a surprise for me has turned into a feeling of unease.

"Do you think I am prejudiced?" I ask.

Her brows knit into a frown.

"Do you remember my reaction when you said Sarah is Chinese?"

"Uh-huh."

"Would I have reacted differently if she had been an East Indian from our own community?"

"You had not expected her to be other than one of our own and that is why you were surprised. Don't read more into it."

"Well, aren't you?"

"No, I'm not. I suppose I might have preferred someone from our own community, but she is as much Canadian as our Al and has as much of the Taiwanese Chinese in her as Al has the Zanzibari Indian in him."

We sit in silence.

"You know, Nuri, there is much of you in him."

"And also much that is not me."

"But then we grew up in colonial Zanzibar and I suppose we still carry our inhibitions with us."

I think of the evening many years ago when, as a student and the only Indian passenger on board the ship that sailed from Zanzibar to England, I first entered the dining room. All faces turned to look unseeing in my direction, then turned back to their plates, as I was directed by the Indian waiter to the lone table reserved for me for the entire month-long journey.

"Yes," I say. "He has none of the inhibitions I had at his age."

I look at her.

"Are you worried, then, that Sarah is not even East Indian?" Her eyes fixed on me.

"No, I'm not worried. I am happy for him and for Sarah. There is nothing I can point to about Al or Sarah that is the cause of the way I feel. Which is what I cannot understand."

I look at her. Her face relaxes into a smile as she takes my hand into hers and squeezes it.

"Just a thought, Nuri. Why not bring it up when you next visit Bapa?"

Bapa, who must be in his eighties, lives in an apartment near our mosque next door to his son and daughter-in-law. He was the first person Mother went to pay her respects to whenever she visited Calgary. I drop in on him about once a month, often to discuss the different ways in which particular texts of our *ginanic* or devotional literature can be plausibly interpreted. Grandma certainly held him in high regard back in Zanzibar because of his extensive reading, which she believed was not confined to our religious texts, though Grandfather thought Bapa talked too much and would retire early to bed on the nights he came to see Grandma.

As always, Bapa begins by asking after my brother Sham who is now a director of an insurance company and whose son practises medicine, and also about my sister Faiza whose daughter will graduate in English this year.

"And our Al?"

"He should be here in a day or two for his summer vacation."

"Seems like yesterday that our Al was a mere toddler, just as you were when I started visiting your grandmother in your father's shop in Zanzibar on Fridays. I don't suppose you remember."

"How could I forget, Bapa? Grandma's arguments and your counter-arguments – though I did not understand much of what either of you said."

I do not tell him that my siblings and I thought he monopolized the conversation or that we found his gesticulations mesmerizing or that we waited for the moments he would whack his thigh when he thought he had made a point. I do, however, tell him how we looked forward to Fridays when he came to the shop after evening prayers for "a natter and your Grandmother's excellent paan" but not that we all knew his special paan contained nothing but a lump of Grandma's choicest chewing tobacco.

"And I thought you were more interested in my glasses," he laughs.

I laugh in turn, feeling somewhat embarrassed perhaps because I still cannot resist peeking at his old rimless glasses, ever precariously poised to slide down his nose.

He bends forward and asks again, "When did you say our Al is expected?"

"In a day or two, Bapa."

"He is a good boy, Al is."

"But he is different, Bapa."

"Hah, of course he is different, as you are different from your parents, who in turn were different from theirs."

"I ... well ... yes."

He stares at me.

"What's amiss, Nuri? Anything to do with Al?"

"Well, yes and no, Bapa."

I proceed to tell him about Al and Sarah, and how both Nimira and I are happy for them. "And yet, what I do not understand is why I feel the way I do."

"Tell me, Nuri, would you have felt the same way if Sarah were from our own community?"

"Probably not."

"Hmm. You remind me of the way we used to think and feel about our 'Indian-ness' in the forties and fifties in Zanzibar."

"How do you mean?"

"I was one of the fools in those days who argued that we were in danger of diluting our identity, our 'Indian-ness,' whatever those terms mean. I thought that we were becoming more African or more westernized and less Indian."

He pauses.

"'Identity,' 'Indian-ness.' Those are weasel words, Nuri. More like the hot air in the balloon taking those it carries to giddying heights. You can't live in a country long enough and avoid contamination. Yes, Nuri, I am like you, ethnically Indian, but like you, I am also Zanzibari and Canadian. The idea of purity is a myth. So is the idea of a single, all-purpose identity."

"But I still don't quite see how what you say helps me understand the way I feel."

"Think of it this way, Nuri. Human beings are arrogant. We want to see ourselves live on forever through our descendants. When your Grandfather came to Zanzibar from India, he expected to see his children and grandchildren continue to be Indians like him and to have all his values. But we no longer live in that world. If he were to return today to the Indian village he left in the nineteenth century, he would be horrified at what he'd regard as the creeping corruption of western values."

He gives a deep rumbling laugh. "Strange that identity, which implies sameness, is more like an ever-changing process."

When I get back home, I find Nimira waiting for me. We sit up till late at night. She listens in silence to what I have to say and to what I believe are perhaps the beginnings of my understanding of my feeling of unease. Perhaps, I tell her, Bapa is right in suggesting that change need not be disconcerting.

The next day Nimira and I go to the airport to meet Al. We see him beaming at us as he comes down the escalator. He jumps the last few steps, runs toward us, and takes us both into his vast open arms. When he releases us, Nimira takes his face into her hands and kisses him on each cheek. He seems to have grown taller.

On our way home from the airport, Nimira monopolizes Al's attention. Her questions repeat what she asks him every Sunday evening during her long phone calls: about the meals he has, if he avoids fast food, if he attends Friday's communal prayers. I have a feeling near satisfaction at his being subjected to the sort of cross-examination I myself had to endure as a bachelor whenever Mother visited Calgary. Al seems to take it all in his stride and is not in the least bit defensive. "No, I haven't tried your recipe yet." "Yes, I did attend the Friday prayers." "No, Ma Miria's chicken *tikka* lacks the punch yours has." He seems relaxed sitting next to me, turned to Nimira in the back seat asking about dinner. "Yes," she says to his as-yet-unasked question if she has made his favourite dessert, *vipopo*, with creamy coconut sauce that he first had years ago when we took him to Zanzibar to see Mother. At least in his eating habits, I think, he is a Zanzibari. "You are the best, Mom," he laughs.

I know Nimira has stocked up the pantry with all the cholesterol-rich food she usually advises her son against, and in which I am often forbidden to indulge. Macadamia nuts her friend brought from Hawaii, which have been kept hidden from me. Jaggery *paak* full of almonds. Cheese made to Mother's recipe.

And the freezer spilling over with garlic *ladoos*, saffron sprinkled pistachio *kulfi* and beef samosas.

On arriving home, Al goes straight to the fridge and takes out bowls of *channa batata*, *daal bhajias* and coconut chutney. I join him at the table. Nimira helps herself from each of our plates as she prepares masala chai.

When we finish our snack, Nimira goes to the laundry room to empty Al's clothes into the washing machine while he and I stay seated at the table.

"Did Mom tell you I am going to Edmonton next week for volunteer work in an old people's home?"

"Yes, she did. I had a look at their programme. Looks good."

Nimira comes in from the laundry room, one of Al's shirts in hand. "I told you a week's stay with us is too short."

"But I have already signed up, Mom. And I am going to spend the rest the holidays with you, anyway. That includes the drive across the Rockies with you both."

"Still," she pouts, then frowns. As she turns round, she says, "This shirt has got to go, Al."

"No, Mom, that's my favourite."

"One man in this house insisting on his rags is enough," she says as she disappears into the laundry room.

I shake my head, telling Al to let go.

"Mom, I have asked Sarah to stay here for a night before we go to Edmonton." He looks at me and says, "I hope that's okay with you both."

"Of course," Nimira says as she comes back to the kitchen. "We will meet her at last."

"Both of you will like her. But don't subject her to your cross-examination, Mom, though her parents, she thinks, are probably as bad as you are, full of questions."

I think of how, at his age, I would never have dared even to think of inviting a girl home for tea, let alone for a night's stay.

Nimira suggests that on his first day back Al should go to the prayer house and meet some of his old friends. When he returns, we have a meal together. He surprises me with questions about his grandparents. He says he remembers the close feel of Mother's warmth. For the first time, he asks about Zanzibar, about our childhood and about how Nimira and I met.

When we retire for the night, I sit in bed stroking Nimira's back. She seems relaxed and happy. I too am at peace. In a strange way, Al's presence is reassuring. I remember what Bapa said about our wish to live on in our children. Perhaps I should consider the future in terms of the acceptance of change and not the regret of loss. I think of Al's children and the children of his children who will not speak Kutchi or Gujarati. Perhaps the colour of their skin will not be the same as ours. There may well come a time when our descendants will have almost nothing of us in them, so that when asked about their multi-caste, multi-racial origins, they might barely remember that some of their forebears came from Zanzibar and others from India, China, Russia, Ethiopia and, yes, Canada. Perhaps, in their world, there will be no hyphenated persons any more.

Maya

Spring for me this year has begun with a first hike to the Bow River across a little wilderness near Bearspaw. Off the highway three miles from Cochrane I take the meandering trail, which, over the winter, must have lain invisible under the prairie snow, unyielding even to the chinook winds. At the wooden bridge beyond the coulee I turn into a track that leads to the river, my eyes on the not-so-distant Rockies. The gods live in the mountains, Grandma used to say. Her gods inhabited the Himalayas, where in the holy village of Rishikesh, by the perennially nascent Ganges, she said she once saw Lord Krishna meet his friend Narad.

"But they are Hindu gods, aren't they, Grandma?"

She is sitting erect on the linoleum floor, left foot on right thigh, head-cover over her shoulders. She raises her eyebrows.

"And we are Muslims, Grandma."

She sucks in paan juice, staring at me. "Our ancestors were Hindus, then became Muslims," she answers, her eyes still locked into mine. "So we are present Muslims and past Hindus."

"Hindu–Muslims, Grandma."

She nods her solemn nod.

Storytelling was a serious matter for her, and needed to be acted out. When she was evil King Duryodhana she would thump the flat of the right hand, *thaap thaap thaap*, on his thigh, summoning innocent Draupadi to his lap, or she would smile the most alluring smile of the nymph Menaka descending from the heavens to seduce the great sage Vishwamitra. She granted us her performances during holiday nights, usually before family and neighbours sitting on the floor in a semicircle. On the rare occasions when she yielded to my entreaties, I would be privileged to see her perform for me alone and be allowed to interrupt with questions.

I let Grandma alone when she was busy haggling with her customers over bead necklaces and bracelets, or with street vendors over mangoes and eggs. The more important questions – why I should have to memorize our daily prayer when I could read it, or why she insisted on my wearing sandals or shoes every time I went out when none of my friends did – I reserved for early mornings when she prepared her first paan in the shop entrance and when nobody would be expected to interrupt us. "Full of questions is our Nuri today," she would often say. If only I had asked ten times the questions I did. What had impelled her, against Grandfather's wishes, to learn to read and write? Was the bearded *mwalimu*, her teacher, married? Where did they meet? And how did she keep it all a secret for so long in Zanzibar where even a whisper echoed forth into a thousand blabbing tales? I have often wondered why we never ask when we should, only to spend the rest of our lives puzzling over haunting conjectures, particularly when, as in my case, the answers had been so easily forthcoming, even if they were, at times, confusing.

"So how did you choose Mother as Father's bride, Grandma?"
   "I have already told you."
   "Yes, but there were so many girls to choose from, Grandma. How did you decide?"
   "They were all long-braided fourteen, fifteen-year-olds who came to buy beads and berries from me."

"*After school, Grandma?*"

"*Yes, always after school.*"

"*So why did you choose Mother?*"

"*Why, child, don't you like your mother?*"

"*Ow, Grandma, tell me why.*"

"*The way she removed her tinseled topi from her head to put the berries in, some to take home to her mother.*"

"*What else?*"

"*She was soft spoken.*"

"*And?*"

"*And she never raised her eyes.*"

"*But she does now.*"

"*Only when you are naughty.*"

"*Please, Grandma, be serious. Why did you really choose her?*"

She grabs me by my right arm, presses me hard into the softness of her firm chest. I feel the beginnings of laughter in her belly as she bursts forth into a toothless hoot, "Because I knew she would make a good mother for you, hee, hee, hee."

The prairie track now runs by the Bow River. The crunch of my heavy steps reminds me of Narad's long and measured strides by the Ganges, matching Krishna's, as Grandma lay hiding behind the thorny hedge, head covered with her yards-long embroidered velvet, palming a prayer, eavesdropping on the divine conversation so that she could tell her grandchild what the two friends talked about.

"*Krishna, like Narad, is in ochre robes. Anyone with eyes to see can tell they are gods and not your run-of-the-mill holy men. And the one on the left with the white beard flowing down to his waist is Krishna himself.*"

"*But how can you tell who is Krishna? Both have beards and both are in ochre robes.*"

"*By the celestial blue that always surrounds the Lord, that's how.*"

In the story, Narad explains, "I did not want anyone to recognize you, Lord. That is why I prayed that you come in ochre robes. But the beard and the long hair?"

"Embellishments?" Krishna bends backward, laughing as he smacks Narad on the back. "Hah, I thought I might as well go all the way and humour my friend."

"Alone at last, Lord, with you," Narad says. "Phew, the aeons I had to spend in meditation to get you all to myself." He sighs as he lowers his head, raises his hand and moves it across his forehead to wipe away beads of perspiration.

"But gods don't perspire, Grandma."
"So what do you do when you meet the Lord?"
"You show respect, Grandma."
"And how do you show respect?"
"By prostrating."
"Or?"
"Bowing."
"And that is exactly what Narad does. He does not want others to recognize Krishna, so he pretends he is perspiring. And to wipe imaginary beads of perspiration off his forehead, he has to lower his head, in secret obeisance."
"Hmm."

Narad then pleads with Krishna to be let into the secret of maya. "Lord, you know what I want from you," he begs again and again. The Lord knows all that is in the minds of gods and humans, but He does not answer.

"Maya," Narad bleats out the word at last. "Lord, I want to experience maya."

"You already know what maya is, Narad."

"But only as an idea, Lord. If only, Lord, I could experience it as real, the way humans experience the illusion, maya, that their everyday world is real."

"Narad, O Narad. The number of times I have told you. Maya

has been devised for human beings, not for gods. I am telling you, friend, you are better off without such experience."

"Narad insists, the way you do, Nuri," Grandma muffles through her paan-filled mouth. "And the loving Lord gives in."
  "Like you, Grandma," I giggle.
  Her staring eyes are sharp in mock reprimand.

"I must prepare to tell you the full story first," the Lord says. "I warn you, Narad, it is a long story." Narad goes to his knees in gratitude. The Lord looks down at him, smiling.

  "Take my flask, Narad, and get me some water from Ganga Ma before I start."

I walk towards the edge of the Bow River and I imagine Narad dipping Krishna's brass flask into the holy river with a *"Bismillah."*

"Narad calls on Allah?"
  "And why shouldn't a Hindu god call upon Allah?"

With the gurgling flask still under the flowing water, Narad suddenly stops.

  "Help!" he thinks he hears.

  The cry is clear at first, then muffled. Right hand cupped to his ear, Narad listens, eyes squinting into slits.

  "Help."

I sit cross-legged on the riverbank and think of the many different versions of the story. In one, Narad dives into the Ganges with the ochre robe on. In another, his right hand tugs at the imaginary robe on the right shoulder and lets it come folding down as he dives in naked. He saves the drowning woman and swims to the opposite bank because it is the nearer. In remembering the story, I feel I have perhaps changed it, at least the part where Narad emerges from the holy river, the woman clad in a clinging wet *sari* in his arms, her smooth firmness pressing against his. He pants with the pangs of a new stirring within, his first feel of flesh, the agony of a god evolving into a man.

Narad takes the woman home. They walk in silence. She leads the way, the pathless terrain known to her. Narad walks behind, absorbed in the rhythm of her gentle strides. Grandma gave her the name Lila, meaning creation, a game the gods play with human beings. Not that I knew the meaning at the time Grandma told and retold the story.

Word goes round the village that Lila has been found. The villagers come out of their mud houses, Hindu women in *saris* and some in long frocks with *dupatas* over their heads. The women in *shalwar khameez* are Muslims. A profusion of discrete colours greets the couple. Hindu men are clothed in their white *dhotis*, Muslims in their loose pants, white also. Children are in sandals, though some are barefoot, and toddlers are mostly naked.

"She's safe."

"Come, come, our Lila is saved."

"We must celebrate."

"Yes, yes."

In the village square, women form a circle under the stars. They begin the *garba* dance, clapping to the beat, slow at first, then picking it up to keep pace with the drummers. Lila leads the song.

> *To my village*
> *Comes a stranger*
> *One day*
> *My pure butter*
> *Tastes the stranger*
> *That day*

The dance speeds up with the *sheeee* of the *shehnai* and the *dhoom dhoom* of the *dhol*. Narad's eyes are on Lila as she whirls around, in cinnamon blouse, red *sari* an unbroken flutter against her long black braid, perspiration streaking down her wide midriff, exposed, teasing. The dizzying whirl suddenly slows to a crawl and the men in their *dhotis* and loose pants, some in shirts, some bare-chested, some in elaborate white turbans, join in for the stick dance.

How the women came to have multicoloured sticks in their hands or how Narad came to be loin-clothed and so handsomely turbaned are questions I did not think to ask.

The dance picks up speed with the *thak thak* clash of the sticks, men's against women's, Narad's against Lila's, her eyes averted, shy, coquettish. The drum beat is now at its loudest, fastest. *Dhoom dhoom dhoom.* The dancers keep pace. *Thak thak thak.* Faster, faster still. "*Waah, waah,*" shouts of praise from the admiring spectators. The dancers are equal to the drummers. The drummers begin to relent. The beat and the whirling circle slow down.

After the dance, late into the night, Narad walks with Lila's father towards the only brick house in the village. Arm round Narad, the old man says, "We will never be able to repay you for what you have done for our Lila. And for us." Narad's eyes are on Lila who is sitting with her mother on the steps of the entrance to the house, waiting for them. Lila sees them approach, looks down, smiles a shy smile, stands up and, holding the edge of her red *sari* to her face, rushes into the house. Narad becomes aware of his heartbeats.

"It is late and you must stay with us for the night," Narad hears the old man say as they sit next to Lila's mother in purple *sari*, bangles on both arms, *siri* in right nostril.

"Yes, yes, stay the night," she insists. "There's no hurry."

Narad agrees.

He stays another night.

And another.

It is impolite to leave too soon.

On the seventh day, Lila's father takes his place, cross-legged, on the raised platform in the front room facing the village. He dips his pen into the inkpot on the desk and scribbles entries in a large leather-bound book. As Narad enters, the old man removes his glasses and replaces the pen in the penholder.

"Like Grandfather?"

"Yes, beta, just like your Grandfather. Spectacles halfway down the nose, looking all serious and important." She muffles a laugh. I giggle.

Narad sits opposite the old man. Lila's mother joins them, taking her seat next to Narad.

"We are old," Lila's father begins. He looks at his wife. She nods.

"I and Lila's mother have been faithful to our *dharma* and fulfilled all our obligations."

He looks at Narad whose eyes are on the door.

"We have one concern, one parental duty yet unfulfilled."

Narad now looks at the old man.

"Lila," the old man says, nodding.

Narad feels his face flush.

"Lila is a good woman, virtuous. And you are a good man, honest. The whole village agrees that you two are well suited."

The old man pauses, looks at his wife again, waits for her to nod and then continues.

"If you agree, and we believe Lila will also agree, we can start preparations for the wedding."

Narad looks down, nods.

"Then it is settled," the old man says, smiling at his beaming wife. They hear a scratching behind the door. Narad imagines Lila's hand cupped to her ear, listening in on the marriage agreement.

"I will teach you all you need to learn about my business and property so that you can take over. I and Lila's mother will then retire, our *dharma* fulfilled."

"What presents do they get, Grandma?"

"So many wedding gifts for Narad and Lila – ghee, bangles, saris, sandals, tiaras, brass plates, flasks."

"And toys?"

"*Toys come later, beta, when they have children.*"

"*Prem and Premita, the twins, Grandma.*"

"*Yes, beta. That is when they get gifts of toys.*"

"*But there are three children, Grandma.*"

"*How could I forget? Of course, the little Baboo. All beautiful children, obedient, compassionate. Prem and Premita, for Baboo is only a babe, work hard at school and at home, helping their parents keep the house clean and run the business.*"

"*What business, Grandma?*"

"*Like your grandfather's and father's. They import rubber sandals from Korea, cutlery from Japan, silk from China.*"

"*And Cadbury's from England, Grandma.*"

"*Yes, beta, and as they prosper, so does the village. Narad becomes even more important than his father-in-law before him, though they never forget the old man and the old woman. A respected member of the community, they elect Narad MLA and make him president of the Rotary Club. Or is it the Lions Club? I forget.*"

"*Rotary Club, Grandma. Like Father.*"

Every year, on the anniversary of the day Narad rescued Lila, he takes his family for a boat ride on the holy river. This particular anniversary, when Baboo has just turned one, falls on the Night of Shiva, Destroyer of the Universe.

"*Does God really destroy the world, Grandma?*"

"*If the world is maya, must not maya make way for what is real?*"

"*Hmmmm.*"

"*A sudden storm, more sudden than even the tropical one, and incomparably violent, violent as only a malicious demon's anger can make.*" She raises her arms. "*Waves as high as our own Beit-al-Ajaib, the House of Wonders.*" She shakes her hands by her ears. "*Lightning unrelenting in ferocity. Vicious rain winds howling their deafening sooooooo.*"

The boat sinks. Narad sees his children drown, first Prem, then Premita. Narad suffers beyond any human suffering. And then

Lila, with her last born, Baboo, clinging to her breast, as Ganga Ma prepares to receive them: "Naaraad, O my Naraaaa ..." His suffering is beyond the suffering of even the gods. Blood trickling down from eyes pressed hard, Narad raises his arms heavenward. "Krishna, O Krishnaaaa." His wail pierces the three worlds.

And the Lord answers, standing next to Narad near the bank of Ganga Ma. "Did you bring me my flaskful of water?"

Narad flattens himself on the ground, first touches, then kisses, then clings to the Lord's feet. He is incoherent, speaks between his sobs.

"What is he saying, Grandma?"

"Difficult to tell, beta. I think, and I am not sure, what he is saying is that he does not want to experience maya, ever."

"Impossible," I hear myself say aloud as I get up from the riverbank. Grandma, Grandfather, Mother, Father, Sham, Faiza, Mama Ayah, Hamisi, Zanzibar – all maya, illusion? Nimira and Al too?

You are still full of questions, Nuri.

I look round. "Is that you Grandma?" I catch myself asking, feeling foolish.

I look round again. "All our lives, in Zanzibar and Canada and elsewhere, all, all is, was, maya?" I hear myself ask.

So the Muslim remembers the story of the Hindu gods?

"A Hindu-Muslim remembers, Grandma."

Beware the hyphen, *beta*.

"So the past, the present, the future, all is maya, illusion, not real, not reliable?"

Yes, *beta*, but these are your thoughts.

"So your story, what you said about illusion and reality. That too is maya?"

Yes, *beta*.

"And so, unreliable?"

As I look into the mist rising over the Bow River, I think I see Lila's smile.

Acknowledgements

Thank you Karl Siegler for your insightful comments and editing. Thank you always, Aritha van Herk – it all began in your workshops. Natalee Caple – I am forever grateful for your unstinting help. Thank you Caroline Adderson and Sandra Birdsell for your wise guidance and generosity. *Asante*, Yasmin Ladha, for enduring an earlier version and for *gup-chupp* during your visits to Calgary. Thank you Barbara Scott and Gregory Gibson for your careful reading and suggestions. And thank you Fred Stenson for your encouragement and support.

Thank you all for your readings, insight and support over the years – Roberta Rees, Lynn Podgurny, Elizabeth Haynes, Al Donnell, Cathie Dunklee-Donnell, Andrea Davies, Carmen Chan, Adele Megann, Rick Wenman and my English 598 peers (2000–2001) at the University of Calgary.

I would also like to thank the writing programs I participated in over the years – Alexandra Writing Centre, University of Calgary Creative Writing program, Humber College, Markin-Flanagan Writer-in-Residence program and Wired Writing program at the Banff Centre.

And for your support, *asante* always, to my siblings – Nurdin, Shirin, Sultan and Yasmin – and to Rozina Janmohamed.

Versions of some of these stories were published in *Vox* 102; *blue buffalo*; and *Due West – 30 Great Stories from Alberta, Saskatchewan and Manitoba* and broadcast on CBC's *Alberta Anthology*.